Let's TOEIC

可搭配108課綱加深加廣選修課程

根據多益
最新改制題型

NEW TOEIC

新多益

黃金互動16週： 基礎篇 增訂二版

附電子朗讀音檔、解析本、模擬試題

李海碩、張秀帆、多益900團隊 編著
Joseph E. Schier 審定

作者介紹

李海碩

- 學歷:
  國立交通大學教育研究所數位學習組碩士

- 經歷:
  臺中市立東山高級中學英語教師
  ETS認證多益英語測驗專業發展工作坊講師
  葳格國際學校總校長

張秀帆

- 學歷:
  國立政治大學英語教學碩士

- 經歷:
  國立政治大學附屬高級中學英語教師
  ETS認證多益英語測驗專業發展工作坊講師

TOEIC 900團隊

專業的多益教材研發及教學顧問團隊，致力於
推廣英語學習。

三民書局

國家圖書館出版品預行編目資料

新多益黃金互動16週：基礎篇／李海碩,張秀帆,多益
900團隊編著.——增訂二版一刷.——臺北市：三民,
2024
面； 公分.——（Let's TOEIC）

ISBN 978-957-14-7781-7 （平裝）
1. 多益測驗

805.1895   113004274

Let's TOEIC

新多益黃金互動 16 週：基礎篇

編 著 者	李海碩、張秀帆、多益 900 團隊
審 訂	Joseph E. Schier

創 辦 人	劉振強
發 行 人	劉仲傑
出 版 者	三民書局股份有限公司 (成立於 1953 年)

三民網路書店
https://www.sanmin.com.tw

地 址	臺北市復興北路 386 號　　（復北門市）　(02)2500-6600
	臺北市重慶南路一段 61 號（重南門市）　(02)2361-7511
出版日期	初版一刷 2018 年 5 月
	增訂二版一刷 2024 年 5 月
書籍編號	S804550
I S B N	978-957-14-7781-7

作者
序

你覺得世界上最偉大的發明是什麼呢？我覺得是匯率。

匯率，提供的就是一個計算的基準。而外語證照也是如此。每個外語證照都像是一種匯率，計算著外語能力的程度。不同的證照匯率不同，能換算的方式也不一樣。若沒有外語證照，我要用什麼方式來衡量能力的基準呢？從比較好大學畢業的學生，外語能力就一定會比較好嗎？如果這兩個人英文聽起來都很好，也都很能表現自己，我要如何更快速地知道他們的實力差異呢？外語證照提供了一個絕佳的功能，讓我們可以透過快速、具有公信力的過程，提供一個足以表達外語能力的數字。

本書是臺灣教科書史上於 TOEIC 改版之後的第一套從高中到大專院校都適用的教材，願能以拋磚引玉之心，邀請更多先進共同投入語言檢定教學的領域，讓臺灣的學子在離開校園前，能在履歷上放上具有國際公信力的匯率，為自己的未來與競爭力加分。在此在下也希望特別感謝一路上共同協助的作者張秀帆老師，以及一同努力並提供全面完整支持的三民書局。一家公司願意出版學校教材，就是在社會責任與收益的天秤上，無悔選擇了社會責任的道路。在下極度榮幸能在這個過程中參與並提供所知，期待這套書籍能夠為教育的現場帶來更多的可能性。

李海碩

多益測驗，TOEIC 是 Test of English for International Communication 的縮寫，顧名思義，是一個評量「如何將英文運用在日常生活中」的能力測驗。為了讓英文不再只是一個考試科目，為了讓英文成為實際、可運用的溝通工具，《新多益黃金互動 16 週：基礎篇》為老師及學習者量身定做，結合了多益測驗、生活情境、真實語料，成為一本可供教學及自學的多益攻略寶典。藉由書中的教學內容、活動應用及實際試題模擬演練，除了可精進多益成績，更可同時掌握在生活中運用英文的能力，讓英文成為你行遍天下的工具，成為你的能力、你的素養，一舉多得！

十一大情境、實境學習、高頻單字

介紹多益測驗常出現的十一大情境，藉由主題情境衍生出真實狀況、高頻單字、及常見問題，讓學習者能從生活事件中習得單字、片語、對話，就像身歷其境，實際去經歷、體會並應用英文，學習英文不再只是單字之間點與點的學習，而是整個事件的立體情境習得，讓記憶變得容易、學習速度加倍！

單元活動、培養批判思考能力

每單元都有小組或兩人活動的安排，藉由活動討論、問題解決、角色扮演，更精熟每單元的內容，且在活動過程中，試著找出問題、提供解決方法，不再只讀死書，而是藉由自由開放的討論、融會多方回應及建議。讓英文的接觸面更寬廣、更靈活，熟悉更多元的回答方式。當別人問我們 "How are you?"，我們不再只是制式的回答 "I'm fine. Thank you. And you?"

還等什麼？快快跟著《新多益黃金互動 16 週：基礎篇》一起達到你人生的英文高峰！

張秀帆

「學生也考多益？」 這句話是我在教授多益課程時最常聽到的質疑。事實上，高中生與大專院校生考多益證照有三大好處：一，準備多益考試可同時提高學測英文分數；二，多益的語言認證可全球走透透；三，準備多益考試可提升國際溝通力。然而，要成功習得語言，最重要的是好教材，《新多益黃金互動 16 週》能精準掌握多益考試的題型及方向，是一套老師和學生都需要的好教材。

兩位編輯者一張秀帆老師以及李海碩老師一皆是美國教育測驗服務社 (ETS) 官方認證的 TOEIC 師資，他們以多年教授多益課程的經驗，編撰出適合教師上課教學及學生準備考試的教材，與市面上的考題解析完全不同。《新多益黃金互動 16 週》不僅可以提升多益考試成績，更可以讓學生在學習語言時，促進互動及溝通的能力，符合新課綱「溝通、互動」的素養導向。

習得語言、掌握英語優勢，不可僅靠死背單字，最重要的是使用語言，透過同儕間的溝通和互動，才能真正內化英語學習，英語才能真正在國際溝通場合派上用場。《新多益黃金互動 16 週》教材設計許多單字練習及課堂活動，內容貼近生活實用及考試趨勢，讓學生學習英語不再枯燥乏味，讓學習變得立體且雙向溝通，透過這套教材，老師絕對可以協助學生體驗英語學習的豐富性與趣味性。

臺北市立和平高級中學校長　溫宥基

🌐 認識 TOEIC

1 TOEIC 是什麼？

TOEIC 的全名為 Test of English for International Communication，亦即國際溝通英語測驗，旨在測驗非英語母語人士在國際職場上的日常英語溝通能力。

2 TOEIC 測驗內容

多益測驗的情境包含一般商務、製造業、金融、企業發展、辦公室、人事、採購、科技、房地產、旅遊、外食、娛樂、保健。為確保不會有利於或不利於特定考生，多益測驗不會出現需要專業知識才能理解的內容，也不會出現如車禍、末期病症、酗酒、犯罪等較為負面的場景。

3 TOEIC 測驗題型

聽力測驗 共 100 題 考試時間為 45 分鐘		閱讀測驗 共 100 題 考試時間為 75 分鐘	
Part 1	Photographs 照片描述題，共計 6 題	Part 5	Incomplete Sentences 句子填空題，共計 30 題
Part 2	Question-Response 問答題，共計 25 題	Part 6	Text Completion 段落填空題，共計 16 題
Part 3	Conversations 對話題，共計 39 題	Part 7	Single Passage Reading 單篇閱讀測驗，共計 29 題
Part 4	Short Talks 短講題，共計 30 題	Part 7	Multiple Passage Reading 多篇閱讀測驗，共計 25 題 (10 題雙篇閱讀測驗，15 題三篇閱讀測驗)

4 準備 TOEIC 有什麼益處？

1. 增強英文聽力及閱讀能力。
2. 培養資訊整合能力及問題解決能力。
3. 增加對各行各業的探索及對職場文化的認識。
4. 在學習歷程檔案中增加語言能力證明。
5. 提升英文科考試的應試技巧。

1 知道該課主題情境 (Setting) 和焦點題型 (Focus) 後，開始進行暖身活動，熟悉情境。

文中出現的高頻關鍵字彙以粗斜體標記，加強單字記憶。

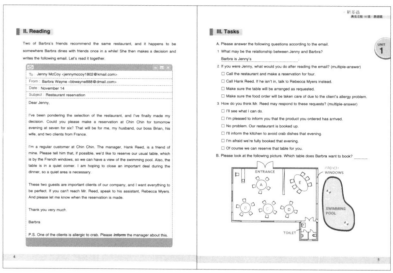

2 進行閱讀任務，透過 TBLT (task-based language teaching) 任務導向的教學方式，自然而然訓練速讀技巧 (skimming & scanning)。

3 認識多益題型及其解題策略，增強聽力測驗或閱讀測驗之應試能力。

4 實戰演練，馬上練習應用剛學到的解題策略。解析本提供解答、聽力腳本及中譯。

🎧 Track　聽力練習的音檔由英、美、澳、加四國口音之錄音員錄製。

5

複習二十個關鍵字彙，
透過該課情境例句掌
握字義。

單字例句皆附美式與英式
口音音檔，學習單字時搭配
音檔以增強聽力測驗時對
單字的辨認能力。

★★★

單字依難、中、易分級，分
別標記為三顆星、兩顆星、
一顆星。學習者可依程度決
定單字學習的優先順序。

6

學習完一至八單元後，挑戰一回多益模擬試題，
感受考試臨場感。

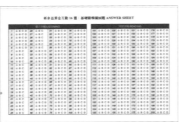

試題本最後一頁為答案卡。
請注意多益考試時不可在題
本上做記號，僅能在答案卡
作答。

分數對照表提供參考分數；
解析提供逐題詳解及中譯。

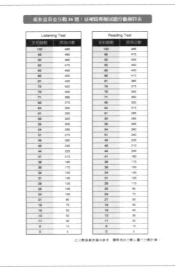

目次
Contents

NEW TOEIC
新多益
黃金互動16週：基礎篇

電子朗讀音檔下載

請先輸入網址或掃描 QR code 進入「三民・東大音檔網」
https://elearning.sanmin.com.tw/Voice/

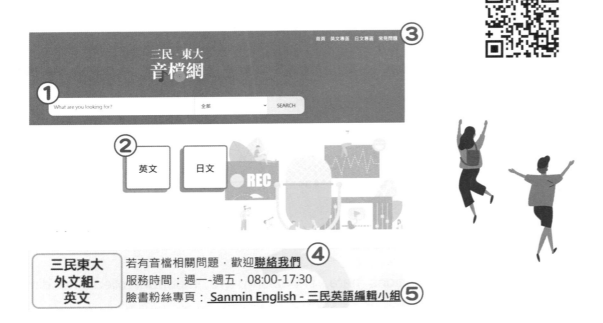

① 輸入本書書名即可找到音檔。請再依提示下載音檔。

② 也可點擊「英文」進入英文專區查找音檔後下載。

③ 若無法順利下載音檔，可至「常見問題」查看相關問題。

④ 若有音檔相關問題，請點擊「聯絡我們」，將盡快為你處理。

⑤ 更多英文新知都在臉書粉絲專頁。

Photo Credits

All pictures in this publication are authorized for use by Depositphotos and Shutterstock.

Restaurant Recommendation and Reservation

I. Warm-up

Ms. Wayne has invited important **clients** to dinner this Friday. She hopes that a fine dining atmosphere will help them close a deal. Thinking about which restaurant to choose, she asks her friends for help on social media. Now please read the following posts.

 Barbra Wayne

2 hours ago

Need some suggestions here. I'm taking two important clients to dinner tomorrow evening and now looking for a fancy, quiet, and **tasteful** restaurant, and of course the one with great service and food. The price is not an issue. Like I said, these two are very important clients. My mission is to make them have an enjoyable evening. Hopefully, with the help of **cuisine**, **beverages**, and some fabulous desserts, I can get the contract signed.

👍❤️😮 26   👍 Like   💬 Comment   ➤ Share

 Bobthesavior

If your clients are meat lovers, my recommendation would be Beefbelly. It has been **catering** for **banquets** since 1978. At Beefbelly, there are **assorted** steaks, sandwiches, and beverages. However, their desserts are not impressive. Yet you can still offer them a delicious meal of meat there!

Like · Reply · 1 hour ago

Miranda Wu

You must take them to Chin Chin. Chin Chin offers healthy, delicious food, and excellent service. It **provides** a wide variety of cuisines to satisfy the tastes of all customers. Also, there's a special menu for **vegetarians**. Above all, the strawberry tart and chocolate mousse are two must-try sweets.

Like · Reply · 52 minutes ago

Pinkaya

I'd also recommend Chin Chin. Their chefs always cook nutritious **recipes**. They don't use **frozen** seafood, so you can always count on the **freshness** of their seafood. And if your clients are **allergic** to anything, just tell them beforehand, and they'll take care of your order. **Reserve** a table before you go. It's usually booked up.

Like · Reply · 11 minutes ago

Think about which restaurant may be the best choice for Ms. Wayne and share your opinion with your classmates!

II. Reading

Two of Barbra's friends recommend the same restaurant, and it happens to be somewhere Barbra dines with friends once in a while! She then makes a decision and writes the following email. Let's read it together.

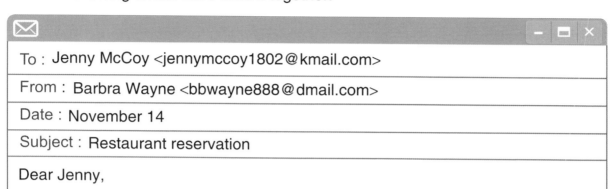

To : Jenny McCoy <jennymccoy1802@kmail.com>

From : Barbra Wayne <bbwayne888@dmail.com>

Date : November 14

Subject : Restaurant reservation

Dear Jenny,

I've been pondering the selection of the restaurant, and I've finally made my decision. Could you please make a reservation at Chin Chin for tomorrow evening at seven for six? That will be for me, my husband, our boss Brian, his wife, and two clients from France.

I'm a regular customer at Chin Chin. The manager, Hank Reed, is a friend of mine. Please tell him that, if possible, we'd like to reserve our usual table, which is by the French windows, so we can have a view of the swimming pool. Also, the table is in a quiet corner. I am hoping to close an important deal during the dinner, so a quiet area is necessary.

These two guests are important clients of our company, and I want everything to be perfect. If you can't reach Mr. Reed, speak to his assistant, Rebecca Myers. And please let me know when the reservation is made.

Thank you very much.

Barbra

P.S. One of the clients is allergic to crab. Please *inform* the manager about this.

III. Tasks

A. Please answer the following questions according to the email.

1. What may be the relationship between Jenny and Barbra?

   Barbra is Jenny's _____.

2. If you were Jenny, what would you do after reading the email? (multiple-answer)

   ☐ Call the restaurant and make a reservation for four.

   ☐ Call Hank Reed. If he isn't in, talk to Rebecca Myers instead.

   ☐ Make sure the table will be arranged as requested.

   ☐ Make sure the food order will be taken care of due to the client's allergy problem.

3. How do you think Mr. Reed may respond to these requests? (multiple-answer)

   ☐ I'll see what I can do.

   ☐ I'm pleased to inform you that the product you ordered has arrived.

   ☐ No problem. Our restaurant is booked up.

   ☐ I'll inform the kitchen to avoid crab dishes that evening.

   ☐ I'm afraid we're fully booked that evening.

   ☐ Of course we can reserve that table for you.

B. Please look at the following picture. Which table does Barbra want to book? _____

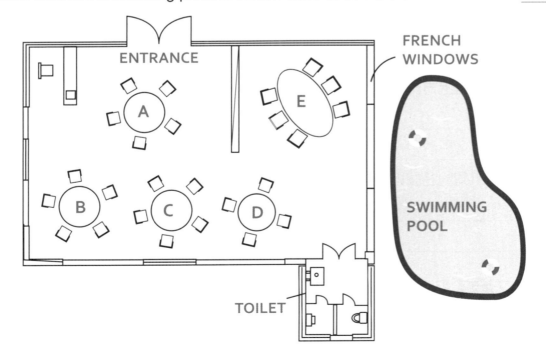

Focus: Listening Test－Photographs

多益聽力測驗第一部分為照片題，共六題，每一題一張照片。考生會聽到四個敘述，必須選出其中一個最能描述該照片的敘述。

題型特色：分為三大類型—「人物動作」、「物品狀態與位置」與「混合型」。

解題關鍵：掌握圖片主題。

★ 第一類：人物動作

> 要掌握圖片主題，即名詞與動詞，最重要的練習就是針對所有能描述圖片的名詞和動詞分開造句。

焦點：名詞與動詞

練習 **1** 請列出描述上方圖片時可使用的名詞與動詞。

✔名詞：_____

✔動詞：_____

練習 **2** 用上方所列的名詞與動詞造句描述圖片。

_____

_____

_____

_____

★ 第二類：物品狀態與位置

> 物品的狀態要靠形容詞，物品的位置則要靠介係詞。所以請試著透過不同的介係詞來描述圖片中各個物品的位置，並用形容詞形容主要物體。此外，因為依然需要描述物品，所以請優先把所有看得見的名詞都先列出來再開始造句唷！

焦點：形容詞與介係詞

練習 1 請列出描述上方圖片時可使用的名詞、形容詞與介係詞。

✔名詞：

✔形容詞：

✔介係詞：

練習 2 用上方所列的名詞、形容詞與介係詞造句描述圖片。

★ 第三類：混合型

焦點：綜合人物類與物品類

練習 **1** 請列出描述上方圖片可使用的詞彙。

　✔名詞：_____

　✔動詞：_____

　✔介係詞：_____

練習 **2** 用上方所列詞彙造句描述圖片。

_____

_____

_____

_____

_____

 Test tip

混合型題目除了人物的動作外還會有豐富的背景資訊。 而錯誤選項常出自於背景資訊， 以本圖而言，"The curtains are open." 即為可能的錯誤選項。

V. Learn by Doing Track-01

請聆聽 1–8 題，選出最能描述照片的選項。

1.

2.

3.

4.

5.

6.

7.

8.

1. recommendation [rɛkəmɛn`deʃn] n. 推薦 ★★★

Have you been in this café before? What's your **recommendation** for coffee and dessert? 你之前來過這間咖啡廳嗎？有推薦的咖啡和甜點嗎？

2. client [`klaɪənt] n. 客戶；顧客 ★★★

We do our best to provide our **clients** with the best service and personal attention.
我們盡其所能對客戶提供最好的服務與體貼入微的照顧。

3. tasteful [`testfl] adj. 有品味的 ★★★

The teahouse is decorated with **tasteful** classical furnishings.
這間茶室以雅致、經典的陳設來裝飾。

4. cuisine [kwɪ`zin] n. 佳餚，料理 ★★★

Tim-Tim chain restaurants are known for their delicious Cantonese **cuisine** and dim sum. Tim-Tim 連鎖餐廳以美味的廣式料理和點心著稱。

5. beverage [`bɛvərɪdʒ] n. 飲料 ★★★

The prices of all the meals in the diner include a **beverage** and a soup.
這間小餐館的餐點價格都包含了飲料和湯。

6. cater [`ketɚ] v. (為…) 提供飲食；迎合 ★★★

Do you know which company will be **catering** Mandy and Jason's wedding reception? 你知道是哪間公司承辦 Mandy 和 Jason 的婚宴嗎？

7. banquet [`bæŋkwɪt] n. 筵席；宴會 ★★★

Juicy Steak will be the restaurant catering for our year-end **banquet**.
Juicy Steak 餐廳將會辦理我們今年望年會的餐點。

8. **assorted** [ə`sɔrtɪd] adj. 各式各樣的

In the newly-opened café at the street corner, there are **assorted** sandwiches, beverages, and cookies. 街角新開張的咖啡廳有各式各樣的三明治、飲料和餅乾。

9. **provide** [prə`vaɪd] v. 提供

The booklet **provides** the information of all the merchandise in the shop.

小冊子提供這間商店裡所有商品的資訊。

10. **vegetarian** [ˌvɛdʒə`tɛrɪən] n. 素食者

Nathan is a **vegetarian** who doesn't eat meat, fish, or other animal products like eggs and milk. Nathan 是個不吃肉、魚、蛋或牛奶等動物產品的素食者。

11. **recipe** [`rɛsəpɪ] n. 食譜

Martha never follows **recipes** exactly when she cooks. She only views them as rough guides. Martha 做菜時從不嚴謹地按照食譜，她只將食譜當作粗略的烹飪引導而已。

12. **frozen** [`frozən] adj. 冰凍的

Frozen vegetables and fresh vegetables have basically the same nutritional value.

冷凍蔬菜與新鮮蔬菜基本上具有相同的營養價值。

13. **freshness** [`frɛʃnɪs] n. 新鮮 ★★★

It's a big challenge to maintain the **freshness** of the seafood served at a restaurant.

要維持餐廳所供應的海鮮的新鮮度是一大挑戰。

14. **allergic** [ə`lɝdʒɪk] adj. 過敏的 ★★★

It's not a good idea to take Bella to a seafood restaurant, for she is **allergic** to shrimps and crab. 帶 Bella 去海鮮餐廳不是個好主意，因為她對蝦蟹過敏。

15. reserve [rɪ`zɝv] v. 預定

Joe has asked his secretary to **reserve** a table for seven at the famous French restaurant. Joe 已經請他的祕書在那間有名的法國餐廳預定七人用餐。

16. inform [ɪn`fɔrm] v. 告知

Please **inform** us two days beforehand if there's any change to your booking. Otherwise, there will be a cancellation fee.

如果預約有任何異動請提前兩天通知我們，否則將會有一筆取消的費用。

17. refreshment [rɪ`frɛʃmənt] n. 茶點

Refreshments will be served during the tea break. 茶點會在午茶休息時間提供。

18. reception [rɪ`sɛpʃən] n. 接待處

Many customers are waiting in the **reception** area for a table.

許多顧客正在接待區候位。

19. cafeteria [kæfə`tɪriə] n. 自助餐廳

David often has a quick lunch at the staff **cafeteria** in order to save more time for work. David 為了省下更多時間工作，常在員工餐廳快速吃午餐。

20. culinary [`kʌlɪˏnɛrɪ] adj. 烹飪的；食物的

From December 9th to 31st, there will be a French **Culinary** Exhibition in Mary's Department Store. 從 12 月 9 日至 31 日，在 Mary 百貨公司將有法國美食展。

2 A Job Interview

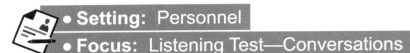

- **Setting:** Personnel
- **Focus:** Listening Test—Conversations

I. Warm-up   Track-04

Ever **Electronics**, a corporation in the USA, is holding an interview for an **assistant** manager. Listen to the conversation and check the **applicants' profiles**. Who is the interviewee?

Applicants' Profiles

Name: Nick Perkins

Current job: Test team leader at Silver Electronics, a middle-sized company, containing 20 employees

Characteristics: quiet, focused, stable

Name: Bob Rose

Current job: Project team leader at Epic Electronics, a small-sized company, containing 6–8 employees

Characteristics: aggressive, optimistic, adaptable

Name: Luis Burton

Current job: Engineer at Electronics Win, a small-sized company, containing 5–8 employees

Characteristics: *independent*, quiet, stable

The interviewee is _____ .

 Why is there no applicant's photo on the profiles?

In most countries, people put their photos on **résumés** to make their profiles more informative. However, in America, Canada, and the United Kingdom, people usually don't do that in case **employers** judge the applicants based on their race.

II. Reading

Green Food Corp. is hoping to **recruit** a new assistant manager too. Let's read the dialogue between their director of human **resources** and a **candidate** for the job.

Ms. Bennet: Good morning, Mr. Lynch. Please have a seat.

Mr. Lynch: Thank you. Just call me James.

Ms. Bennet: OK. My name is Helen Bennet, and I'm the HR director. I see here on your résumé that you're applying for the **position** of assistant manager?

Mr. Lynch: Yes, that's correct.

Ms. Bennet: Can you tell me about your work experience?

Mr. Lynch: Of course. I'm working as a project manager in a middle-sized foods corporation, Joyce Foods Corporation.

Ms. Bennet: Oh, I know Joyce Foods Corp. A small but good company.

Mr. Lynch: That's right. Before that, I worked in the sales department as a team leader for an electronics company. I have had twelve years of working with many different types of businesses.

Ms. Bennet: That's quite impressive. May I ask you why you're interested in our company, Green Food Corp.?

Mr. Lynch: Well, I just think I should make some progress. I've been working at my present job for four years, and it's time for me to move on and look for new challenges. Because your company focuses on customer service, one of my specialties, I think we can make a good match.

Ms. Bennet: OK. In this position, there will be a lot of **opportunities** to work with other people as a team. Do you work well with others?

Mr. Lynch: Yes! I enjoy teamwork.

Ms. Bennet: Good. Lastly, can you tell me why we should hire you?

Mr. Lynch: I'm good at coming up with new project ideas, and I don't mind working overtime when it's necessary.

Ms. Bennet: Well, thank you for coming in today. After interviewing other candidates, I'll get back to you as soon as there's a decision.

Mr. Lynch: Thank you for having me here today. Look forward to hearing from you.

III. Tasks

A. Work with your partner to complete the following application form for James.

Job Application Form

Position Applied for: _____

APPLICANT'S PROFILE

First Name: _____ Last Name: _____

Postal Address: _____ 4693 East Main St., Washington DC 88059 _____

Permanent Address: _____ 4693 East Main St., Washington DC 88059 _____

Phone No.: _____ (855) 633-9879 _____ Office: _____ (855) 639-5151 _____

Email Address: _____ jjlynch@kmail.com _____

Marital Status: _____ Married _____

Present Employer: _____ Joyce Foods Corporation _____

Current Position: _____

Total Experience: _____ (years)

Present Salary: _3000 USD (per month)_

Expected Salary:* _____ (per month)

* There's no standard answer for the blank for "Expected Salary." Please note that the expected salary would be normally higher than the present one.

B. According to James' application form and his performance in the job interview, would you hire him if you were Helen? Discuss with your partner!

IV. Test Tactics

Focus: Listening Test－Conversations

新制多益的對話題部分共有 13 組兩人或三人間的簡短對話，每組對話有三題理解測驗。

題型特色： 1.問題與選項皆印於題本。

2.對話只會播放一次，每組對話與對話間隔 30 秒。

解題關鍵：對話一播放結束，不要聆聽接下來播放的問題，而要在這 30 秒間隔直接自行作答，然後立刻速讀下一題組題目，以此掌握下一組對話播放時需要專注的關鍵訊息。

以下方試題為例：

1. What is this conversation mainly about?

   (A) Discussing where to have a study group

   (B) A meeting about a job *vacancy*

   (C) Handling customer complaints

   (D) Resolving a conflict between two students

2. What does the woman say about the room on floor 2?

   (A) It is being renovated.

   (B) It is crowded with students.

   (C) It is already booked.

   (D) It is closed today.

3. What does the man say he will do this afternoon?

   (A) Meet up with the applicants

   (B) Listen to others' opinions

   (C) *Submit* his comments

   (D) Share his research findings

Test tip

> 速讀時先看三個題幹，還有時間再看選項。不要因為求速而導致沒有確實掌握問題主旨。

在對話播放以前，速讀題目時應掌握問題關鍵：

題目關鍵字		聽力要點
mainly about	➡	聽出全篇對話主題
the room on floor 2	➡	細節一：關於二樓的房間
what he will do this afternoon	➡	細節二：關於男子下午會做的事

現在請根據上述聽力要點來聆聽這則對話，請試著一邊聆聽，一邊作答。 Track-05

剛剛在聆聽過程中，根據聽力要點所掌握的關鍵訊息：

聽力要點	關鍵訊息
聽出全篇對話主題	➡ study group
細節一：關於二樓的房間	➡ That room has been booked.
細節二：關於男子下午會做什麼	➡ I'll share my findings with you this afternoon.

UNIT
2

因此正確答案為：1. ___A___　2. ___C___　3. ___D___

現在請用下方題組練習此解題技巧。4–6 題組對話一播放結束，請盡速完成作答，然後緊接著速讀 7–9 題組題目。請注意，7–9 題組對話一旦開始播放就要專心聆聽！ Track-06

4. Why is the man calling?

   (A) He wants French and Spanish lessons.

   (B) He is looking for employees who speak foreign languages.

   (C) He is looking for a job.

   (D) He needs help writing a résumé.

5. Which language does the man probably speak better?

   (A) French

   (B) Spanish

   (C) Both about equally

   (D) Neither very well

6. What does the woman say that the man will have to do?

   (A) Translate a document into French

   (B) Show that he can speak French

   (C) Conduct an interview in Spanish

   (D) Speak Spanish well

7. What is wrong with the man's computer?

   (A) The screen is broken.

   (B) The computer turns on by itself.

   (C) The computer shuts down by itself.

   (D) The keyboard needs repairing.

8. What did the man read in the company's brochure?

   (A) Melon computers are on sale.

   (B) They are selling used keyboards.

   (C) They are selling Tokuba computers at discounted prices.

   (D) They are launching a new Tokuba computer.

9. What is the woman about to do?

   (A) Discuss getting a Tokuba for the man

   (B) Demonstrate how to use advanced features

   (C) Bargain the price with the man

   (D) Look for a newer laptop model

V. Learn by Doing Track-07

請聽以下 1-15 題的對話並回答問題。

1. What is the man worried about?

   (A) Not getting to the hotel on time

   (B) Not finding a parking spot

   (C) Not understanding the map

   (D) Having to pay an additional fee

2. What did the woman forget to bring?

   (A) A picture of the hotel

   (B) The address of the hotel

   (C) Directions to the hotel

   (D) Money to stay in the hotel

3. Why does the man want to stop?

   (A) To buy a new map

   (B) To call the hotel

   (C) To eat some dinner

   (D) To ask for some assistance

4. Who is Mr. Xiao?

   (A) Construction worker

   (B) Manager of the project

   (C) Secretary

   (D) Purchasing manager

5. What problem does Ms. Andrews encounter?

   (A) She can't figure out how to design the bank.

   (B) A measurement is incorrect.

   (C) She doesn't have the blueprint.

   (D) She ordered wrong building materials.

6. What does Ms. Andrews have to do?

   (A) Redraw the blueprint

   (B) Keep looking for the drawing

   (C) Redesign the first and second floors

   (D) Visit Mr. Xiao's office tomorrow

7. Who is scheduled to visit the manufacturer?

(A) The COO of a painting company

(B) The CEO of a law firm

(C) The CEO of a manufacturing company

(D) The COO of a marketing company

8. Why does the man suggest another day?

(A) They are planning on painting the factory.

(B) They will inspect the production machinery.

(C) They are touring the production line.

(D) They are having a confidential meeting.

9. What will the woman probably do next?

(A) Ask the COO if he can come next Thursday

(B) Cancel the COO's visit

(C) Call the marketing company's CEO

(D) Visit the marketing company

10. What was the man's presentation about?

(A) Electronic devices

(B) Human resources

(C) Sales

(D) Administration

11. What positive feedback did the people give?

(A) The presentation was helpful.

(B) The examples were powerful.

(C) The speech was well-organized.

(D) The man was confident.

12. What improvement does the man want to make?

(A) Adjust his gestures

(B) Give more key points

(C) Speak faster

(D) Use fewer gestures

 Test tip

多益新制考題的對話題中，多數題組為一男一女兩人對話，但有少數題組為兩男一女或兩女一男三人對話。聆聽時請掌握①對話目的②對話者彼此的關係③並特別留意性別僅有一位的說話者所提供的資訊，如此就能處理三人對話題中較大的資訊量。

Article title	Deadline
Mammoth Mutations	1/11
Hawaii Legends	4/12
Discovering Desert Islands	3/10
The Hidden World	3/10

13. Which article needs to be lengthened?

(A) "Mammoth Mutations"

(B) "Hawaii Legends"

(C) "Discovering Desert Islands"

(D) "The Hidden World"

14. Look at the graphic. Which article's deadline will be adjusted?

(A) "The Hidden World"

(B) "Discovering Desert Islands"

(C) "Hawaii Legends"

(D) "Mammoth Mutations"

15. What will the woman send the man?

(A) A new article on mammoth mutations

(B) Pictures of desert islands

(C) Information on "The Hidden World"

(D) Ideas for an article on Hawaii

 Test tip

多益新制考題新增圖表題。速讀時，仍應先閱讀三題題幹，若看到題幹出現 "Look at the graphic." 則表示該題需要搭配圖表資訊。

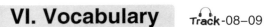 

VI. Vocabulary Track-08-09

---

1. **personnel** [ˌpɝsəˈnɛl] n. 職員；人事部門

This part of the factory is a restricted area, open to authorized **personnel** only.

工廠的這部分是管制區域，僅開放給授權職員進入。

---

2. **electronics** [ɪˌlɛkˈtrɑnɪks] n. 電子技術；電子學

Frank is going to apply for the marketing manager position in E&E **Electronics** Company. Frank 要應徵 E&E 電子公司的市場部經理一職。

---

3. **assistant** [əˈsɪstənt] n. 助理；助手

The chairman himself isn't in today. His personal **assistant** could help you.

董事長今天不在，他的私人助理可以協助你。

---

4. **applicant** [ˈæplɪkənt] n. 申請者

There are 20 **applicants** for this position of secretary. It's very competitive.

有二十位申請者來應徵這個祕書職位，非常競爭。

---

5. **profile** [ˈprofaɪl] n. 簡介；個人檔案

Natalie was called for a job interview soon after she updated her **profile** on the job board. Natalie 更新求職網站上的個人簡介後不久就收到面試通知。

---

6. **independent** [ˌɪndɪˈpɛndənt] adj. 獨立的

Gary has been financially **independent** for years. He always budgets his salary carefully. Gary 已經經濟獨立好幾年了，他總是謹慎使用自己的薪水。

---

7. **résumé** [ˈrɛzəme] n. 履歷

Daniel sent his **résumé** to at least 15 companies and finally got an interview invitation. Daniel 至少向十五家公司投了履歷，終於得到面試邀約。

UNIT **2**

8. employer [ɪm`plɔɪɚ] n. 雇主

Many **employers** believe that hands-on experience is equally important as academic qualifications.　許多雇主相信實際經驗與學歷同等重要。

9. recruit [rɪ`krut] v. 招募

Due to financial difficulties, the company didn't **recruit** new staff this year.

由於財務困難，公司今年沒有招聘新員工。

10. resource [`rɪsors] n. 資源

Our company's most valuable **resource** is the commitment of our employees.

我們公司最有價值的資產就是員工的全力投入。

11. candidate [`kændɪdet] n. 求職應徵者；候選人

This afternoon, we interviewed a few strong **candidates** for this position.

今天下午，我們面試了一些來應徵這個職位的實力堅強的應徵者。

12. position [pə`zɪʃən] n. 職位；位置

It's quite awkward between Jeff and me right now, for we are competing for the same **position** in QG Electronics.

現在 Jeff 和我有些尷尬，因為我們兩個一起競爭 QG 電子公司的同一職位。

13. opportunity [ˌɑpɚ`tjunətɪ] n. 機會 ★★★

Job **opportunities** for graduates are quite limited at present.

大學畢業生目前的工作機會相當有限。

14. permanent [`pɝmənənt] adj. 固定的；永久的 ★★★

Jeremy hopes that he can find a **permanent** job so that he can stop buzzing around the city seeking jobs.

Jeremy 希望能找到一份固定的工作，這樣他才不用一直在城市裡跑東跑西地找工作。

15. expect [ɪk`spɛkt] v. 預期

They **expected** a lot of applicants for the job, and yet just a few came to the interview.　他們預期有許多人來應徵這個工作，然而只有少數人來面試而已。

16. vacancy [`vekənsi] n. 職缺

There is a **vacancy** for a cashier at Goody Mart. Are you interested?
Goody Mart 有個收銀員的職缺，你有興趣嗎？

17. submit [səb`mɪt] v. 提交

Applicants should **submit** their résumés before December 5th.
應徵者應該在十二月五日前提交履歷表。

18. ethic [`ɛθɪk] n. 道德；行為準則

Luke is working on strengthening the work **ethic** at his company, since it plays a crucial role in efficiently achieving a company's goals.
Luke 正努力加強他公司內部的工作守則，因為這對於一間公司能有效率地達成目標扮演著重要的角色。

19. proficiency [prə`fɪʃənsɪ] n. 熟練程度；精通

Candidates for the senior engineer's position are required to demonstrate a high level of technical **proficiency**.
來應徵高級工程師一職的人必須要展現高階的技術水平。

20. consideration [kən͵sɪdə`reʃən] n. 考慮；思考

Joseph's proposal was rejected at the meeting this afternoon. The boss thought it needed further **consideration**.
Joseph 的提案在今天下午的會議中被駁回，老闆認為該提案有待進一步考慮。

Buying Stationery

● Setting: Purchasing
● Focus: Listening Test—Question-Response

I. Warm-up

Scott is the purchasing agent at Robin & Robert Medical. It's time for the annual **purchase**. Scott is now filling out a purchase order.

No.	Item *Description*	Quantity	Unit Price (USD)	Total (USD)
	Robin & Robert Medical **Stationery Purchase Order**			
1	PEN-BLUE	500		
2	PENCIL-2B	250		
3	STAPLER	100		
4	LABELS	40 packs		
5	PAPER-A4	200 packs		

Before Scott writes the unit price and total, he needs to decide where he is going to purchase these **items**. He finds that there are two stationery stores having a sale. Please check out the two flyers below and help Scott make the decision.

Which one would you choose and why? Tell your classmates!

II. Reading

Maya is an employee of Venus Press. Here is a notice just placed on their staff bulletin board. Let's read it together with her!

Notice to All Employees

Good news! Venus Press has had a 20% increase in sales this year and has achieved something incredible: having our annual sales of more than 20 million dollars! As a reward for your efforts and devotion, orders of office stationery will now be placed on a monthly basis.

The new arrangements will be as follows:

- The assistant of each department will place the orders through the purchasing department by the 5th of every month.
- Each department may place up to 10 orders / 500 USD per month.
- Each employee should fill out the purchase form to inform the assistant as to his or her needs.
- The department with the fewest orders of the year will *obtain* gift *vouchers* at Mary's department store.

The arrangements above are *provisional*. After the trial period of three months, we will then review the policy to see if any *alterations* are needed.

The Purchasing Department

III. Tasks

Maya is discussing the new arrangements with one of her colleagues. If you were Maya, what would you say? What may be the pros and cons of this policy? Please discuss with your classmates and write your opinion below.

Colleague: Wow! We'll have plenty of pens and pencils and folders and everything! The policy is awesome!

Maya: Yes, the policy . . .

_____

_____

_____

However, I'm afraid there might be a problem if . . .

_____

_____

IV. Test Tactics

Focus: Listening Test－Question-Response

多益問答題共 25 題。考生會先聽到一個問題或一句陳述 (a question or a statement)，再聽到三個回應選項，最後須選出最適當的回應。問題及選項均只會播放一次。

題型特色： 1. 問題與選項均不印於題本上，需完全憑藉聽力作答。題本上僅印有 "Mark your answer on your answer sheet."。

2. 常見的問句包含 5W1H 以及 Which 及 Whom、Yes/No 問句、及附加問句；常見的陳述包含肯定句及否定句。

解題關鍵： 1. 每字每句不漏聽。

2. 掌握問題句型並能靈活應對。

請用以下「聽寫、預測、回推」三階段式練習來訓練自己的解題能力。

Step 1 聽寫練習　Track-10

若要具備把題目與選項都清晰聽出來的能力，最好的訓練方式即「聽寫」。請聆聽下方試題，並兩人一組，合作把問題與選項逐字聽寫在表格中，並在最適當的選項劃記。

	Question	
1.	**Responses**	Ⓐ
		Ⓑ
		Ⓒ
2.	Question	
	Responses	Ⓐ
		Ⓑ
		Ⓒ
3.	Question	
	Responses	Ⓐ
		Ⓑ
		Ⓒ

UNIT **3**

Step 2 預測練習

「聽問句，想答句」的練習能訓練出靈活應對問題的能力。練習時若能預測到越多可能的回答，考試時愈容易辨認出正確的選項。請用下方試題來做預測練習。

練習步驟： 1. 聽問句，將問句聽寫在 Question 欄位。

2. 兩人一組想出至少三個可能的答句，寫在 Possible Responses 欄位。

3. 聽選項，聽寫在 Answer 欄位並在最適當的選項上劃記。

4. 對答案，並比較正確答案是否接近自己的預測。

1. 〈範例〉	**Question**	Did you get lots of bargains at the clearance sale? Track-11
	Possible Responses	Yes, tons of good stuff!
		Yes, they were 70% off!
		No, the prices were still too high.
	Answer	Ⓐ ● Ⓒ Correct answer: Yes, everything was half-price.
2.	**Question**	Track-12

	Possible Responses	
	Answer	Ⓐ Ⓑ Ⓒ Correct answer: Track-13
	Question	Track-14
3.	Possible Responses	
	Answer	Ⓐ Ⓑ Ⓒ Correct answer: Track-15

Step 3 回推練習

「聽答句，想問句」的回推練習則能加強對問題句型的掌握能力。

練習步驟： 1. 聆聽答句 b-i，聽寫在 Response 欄位。   Track-16

        2. 兩人一組想出至少一個答句可能對應的問句，寫在 Possible Question 欄位。

        3. 聆聽 1–3 題，在最適當的選項上劃記。

Response	Possible Question
a. In another 30 minutes. (範例)	When will you come? When will the train arrive?
b.	
c.	
d.	
e.	
f.	
g.	
h.	
i.	

1. Mark your answer on your answer sheet.

2. Mark your answer on your answer sheet.

3. Mark your answer on your answer sheet.

1	Ⓐ Ⓑ Ⓒ
2	Ⓐ Ⓑ Ⓒ
3	Ⓐ Ⓑ Ⓒ

 Track-17

Test tip

四大類基本問題句型
1. 詢問資訊：When / How long. . . ?
   What / Where / Who / Whom / Which /
   Why / How. . . ?
   Do you know. . . ?
   Could you tell me. . . ?
2. 徵詢意見：What would you say about. . . ?
   What do you think about. . . ?
   What's your opinion of. . . ?
3. 請求：Could you / Can I / May I. . . ?
   Would you mind if. . . ?
4. 邀約：Would you like to. . . ?

UNIT 3

V. Learn by Doing Track-18

請聽以下 1–10 題，選出最適當的回應選項。

1. Mark your answer on your answer sheet.

2. Mark your answer on your answer sheet.

3. Mark your answer on your answer sheet.

4. Mark your answer on your answer sheet.

5. Mark your answer on your answer sheet.

6. Mark your answer on your answer sheet.

7. Mark your answer on your answer sheet.

8. Mark your answer on your answer sheet.

9. Mark your answer on your answer sheet.

10. Mark your answer on your answer sheet.

1	Ⓐ Ⓑ Ⓒ	6	Ⓐ Ⓑ Ⓒ
2	Ⓐ Ⓑ Ⓒ	7	Ⓐ Ⓑ Ⓒ
3	Ⓐ Ⓑ Ⓒ	8	Ⓐ Ⓑ Ⓒ
4	Ⓐ Ⓑ Ⓒ	9	Ⓐ Ⓑ Ⓒ
5	Ⓐ Ⓑ Ⓒ	10	Ⓐ Ⓑ Ⓒ

1. **purchase** [`pɝtʃəs] n. 購買；採購

Skylar is used to paying for her **purchases** by credit card.

Skylar 習慣以信用卡購物。

2. **description** [dɪ`skrɪpʃən] n. 描述，敘述

Just write a rough **description** of the items you would like to buy on the purchase order sheet. 在購物訂單表上寫下你想購買的物品的簡略描述即可。

3. **item** [`aɪtəm] n. 項目；物品

The ladies in the store are going through the clothes on sale **item** by **item.**

店裡的女子們一件件地翻看打折的衣服。

4. **clearance sale** [`klɪrəns sel] n. 清倉大拍賣

The clothing store is holding a **clearance sale** to get rid of its summer items.

衣服店正舉辦清倉大拍賣來出清夏季商品。

5. **goods** [gʊdz] n. 商品；貨物

During this weekend, there will be a 40% discount on all the **goods** in the shop.

這個週末，這間商店裡的全部商品都有六折優惠。

6. **wholesale** [`hol͵sel] adj. 批發的

Big Buddy sells sporting goods at **wholesale** prices.

Big Buddy 以批發價販售運動用品。

7. **linger** [`lɪŋgɚ] v. 逗留，徘徊

People can't help **lingering** in Vivian's Boutique, for the goods there are delicate.

人們忍不住流連在 Vivian 的精品小店裡，因為裡面的商品很精緻。

8. anniversary sale [ˌænəˈvɝsərɪ sel] n. 週年慶促銷

Davis' Department Store is offering up to 80% off on cosmetics in the **anniversary sale**.　Davis 百貨公司正在週年慶促銷活動中推出化妝品最低兩折的折扣。

9. stock [stɑk] n. 存貨；庫存

The Toy World is having a big sale on their last year's **stock**.
The Toy World 正舉行去年存貨的大拍賣。

UNIT
3

10. bulk [bʌlk] n. 大量

Offices often buy paper and other stationery in **bulk** to keep costs down.

辦公室通常都會大量購買紙張及其他文具以減少成本開銷。

11. merchandise [ˈmɝtʃənˌdaɪz] n. (總稱) 商品

There are few complaints about the **merchandise** from our company because each of our products is of high quality.

消費者對我們公司的商品幾乎沒有抱怨，因為我們每項產品都是高品質的。

12. obtain [əbˈten] v. 得到，獲得

That man is the lucky 1000th visitor to our department store today! He will **obtain** a $1,000 prize.　那位男士是我們百貨公司本日幸運的第一千名訪客，他將獲得一千元獎金。

13. voucher [ˈvaʊtʃɚ] n. 商品券；優惠券

The **vouchers** are valid between January and November. Please use them before they expire.　這些優惠券的有效期間為一月到十一月，請在到期前使用。

14. provisional [prəˈvɪʒənl] adj. 暫定的

The date of our product launch set in the meeting is only **provisional**. The exact date is not confirmed yet.
會議中訂定的產品發表會日期只是暫定的，實際日期還沒有確定。

15. alteration [ˌɔltəˈreʃən] n. 變更；改變

Since the budget of our project has been cut by 30%, some **alterations** to our original plans are necessary.

既然我們計畫的預算被砍了 30%，原本的安排就有必要做些改變。

16. refund [ˈriˌfʌnd] n. 退款

Consumers can take the purchased item back to the store and ask for a **refund** within seven days of the purchase.

消費者可以在購物後七天內將購買的商品拿回商店要求退費。

17. appliance [əˈplaɪəns] n. 設備；器具

We can use our year-end bonuses to purchase some new domestic **appliances**.

我們可以用我們的年終獎金採買一些新的家用電器。

18. warranty [ˈwɔrəntɪ] n. 保固；保證書

The laptop **warranty** does not cover any damage caused by misuse, accidents, or neglect.　這部筆電的保固不包含錯誤使用、意外或疏忽造成的損壞。

19. manual [ˈmænjʊəl] n. 手冊；指南

Adam was shocked when he saw the color laser printer's 800-page user **manual**.

Adam 看到雷射印表機八百頁的使用指南時嚇了一跳。

20. consumer behavior [kənˈsumɚ bɪˈhevjɚ] n. 消費者行為

The recession will definitely affect **consumer behavior**. The consumers may become more cautious and price-conscious.

經濟衰退一定會影響消費者行為，消費者會變得更謹慎且更在意價格。

4 Filling out the Expense Report Form

- **Setting:** Office
- **Focus:** Reading Test—Single Passage Reading

I. Warm-up

Adam just took over the job as the Chief Executive Officer's secretary. The former secretary gave him something with a written manual. Please read the *instruction* manual together with him.

All the files, especially the confidential ones, need to be stored both in the PC on your desk AND in this external hard drive as a backup. This hard drive has a large capacity up to 3TB. You can connect it to your PC through a USB 2.0 or USB 3.0 connector. Though it can store an extensive range of files, please store files about work only.

Please handle the hard drive carefully to avoid hardware damage and data loss. And before using it, please read the following instructions carefully!

✓ Do NOT move the drive while it is operating or connected to the computer.

✓ When running for a long period of time, like 1 hour, the hard drive may become very warm. Don't worry. This is completely normal, and its advanced design can help cool it down quickly.

✓ Do NOT attempt to open the drive's case.

✓ Do NOT stack anything on the top of the drive or set the drive on its side. Either action may cause damage to it.

✓ Check the drive and remove unnecessary files periodically.

Good luck with your new job!

Below are some pieces of office equipment. Write down what they are and find out which is the one Adam got from the former secretary.

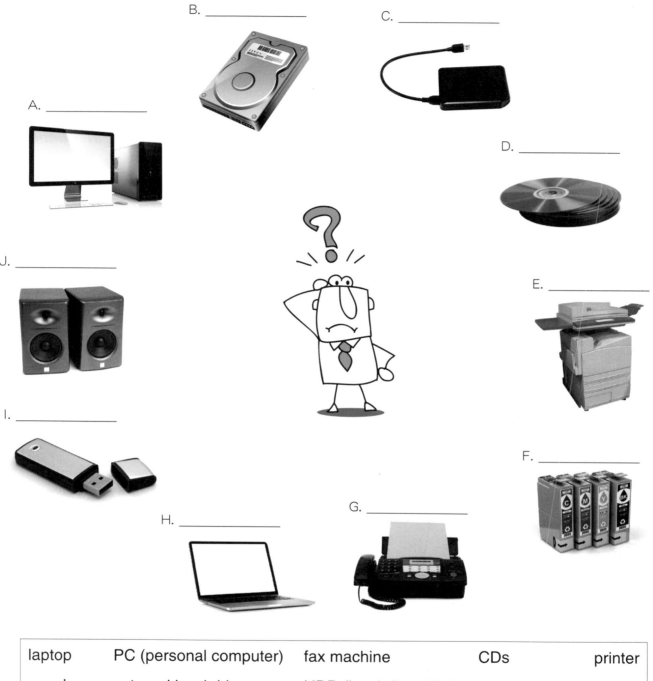

B. _____

C. _____

A. _____

D. _____

J. _____

E. _____

I. _____

F. _____

H. _____

G. _____

| laptop | PC (personal computer) | fax machine | CDs | printer |
| speakers | external hard drive | HDD (hard disc drive) | ink cartridges | USB |

The former secretary gave Adam _____ .

II. Reading

Abraham is a member of staff of Brian's Brain Co. The following is an email he just received.

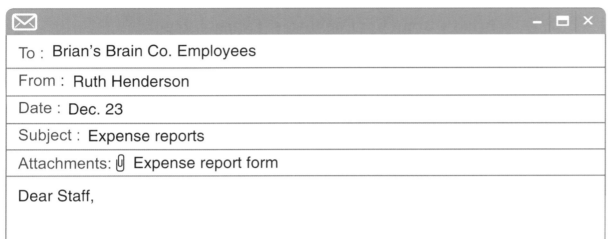

UNIT
4

To : Brian's Brain Co. Employees

From : Ruth Henderson

Date : Dec. 23

Subject : Expense reports

Attachments: 📎 Expense report form

Dear Staff,

A quick and **urgent** reminder to **notify** you that you MUST submit your expense reports by the end of this year. Please make sure that you submit all the receipts of your purchases along with the report. Except entertainment expenses, expenses of travel, **accommodation**, and food can all be listed in the report. Do remember to fill in your employee identification number when filling out the report so as to speed up the process. You'll be **reimbursed** by the end of next month.

Please find the expense report form attached. After filling it out, leave it and your receipts on my desk, or give them to any member of the Cashier Section by Dec. 31st. Last but not least, don't forget to keep a **duplicate** of the report for yourself.

Thank you, and Happy New Year!

Ruth Henderson
Chief of the Cashier Section

III. Tasks

After reading the email, please help Abraham **complete** his expense report by checking his employee ID card and receipts below.

Brian's Brain Co. Employees' Expense Report

Purpose: _Software testing for banks_   Statement Number: 45015864582

Employee Information:

Name: _____   Employee ID Number: _____

Department: _____   Position: _____

Date	Description	Hotel	Transport	Meals
	Hotel (1 night)			
	Dinner			
			TOTAL	

Abraham Lucas

Employee ID: TS890443227

Department: Technology

Position: Software Engineer

Brian's Brain Co.

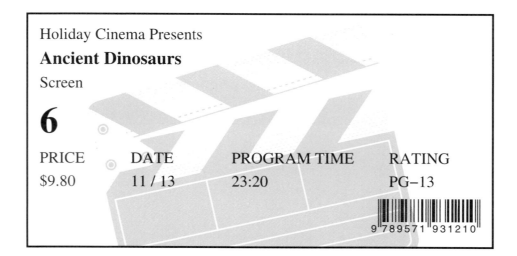

Holiday Cinema Presents
Ancient Dinosaurs
Screen

6

PRICE   DATE   PROGRAM TIME   RATING
$9.80   11 / 13   23:20   PG–13

9 789571 931210

Hotel Star Vacation

Resort & Spa

Abraham Lucas
557 Golden Road
Bakersfield, California 93309

Arrival: 11 / 13
Departure: 11 / 14
Room: 614, 616

Date	Description	Debit	Credit
11/13	Room	140.00	
11/13	Room Tax (8%)*Room	11.20	
11/13	Room	140.00	
11/13	Room Tax (8%)*Room	11.20	
11/14	Laundry Service	15.00	
			317.40

Balance: $0

PAID IN FULL

Signature: _____Abraham Lucas_____

Thank you for being our guest! We look forward to accommodating you again.

Cyd's Deli Café

Date: 11 / 13

Item	Qty	Price	Total
T-bone Steak	2	30.00	60.00
Fanta Orange	1	5.50	5.50
Mojito	1	12.50	12.50
		SUB TOTAL	78.00
		TAX	7.80
		TOTAL	85.80

UNIT
4

IV. Test Tactics

Focus: Reading Test—Single Passage Reading

新制多益的閱讀部分中，單篇閱讀測驗共有 29 題。考生會先閱讀一段文字，如新聞、廣告、信件、簡訊、意見調查等不同文類，接著回答二至四題閱讀理解測驗。

題型特色：測驗資訊理解能力與閱讀速度。

解題關鍵：採用 SSA 閱讀測驗解題步驟 (Skim the questions. → Scan the text. → Answer the questions.) 快速作答。

以下方試題為例：

Questions 1–2 refer to the following chain of text **messages**.

Nicole	10:15 A.M.
Hello Mr. Nicholson, I'm Nicole, the general manager of Entertainment Seventeen. In our **correspondence** via email, we didn't get to thank you for the extensive research you are willing to do for our company. I'm sure the research results will be very **informative** for us.	
Robert	10:16 A.M.
The pleasure is mine. I hope I can be of service to your company. The work I will do is strictly for your company, and needs to be kept highly confidential. Please make sure that it doesn't fall into the hands of another company.	
Nicole	10:18 A.M.
Sure, we'll keep that in mind. Would you please come in and sign some documents regarding this project? It's quite urgent. We will need your signature. We will also sign a confidentiality **agreement**, so you know we are serious about this.	
Robert	10:21 A.M.
OK. I'll be in tomorrow morning before 10:00.	

1. Who is Robert?

   (A) Nicole's co-worker

   (B) A research consultant

   (C) A travel agent

   (D) A CEO

2. At 10:16 A.M., what does Robert most likely mean when he writes "The pleasure is mine"?

   (A) He got the credit for working on research.

   (B) It's his pleasure to serve the company.

   (C) He wants to be pleased by being paid more.

   (D) He needs more praise for his hard work.

解題步驟如下圖：

Skim the questions.
略讀問題，掌握閱讀要點

閱讀要點：1. Robert 是誰　2. "The pleasure is mine" 含意為何

Scan the text.
掃描文章，根據閱讀要點取得關鍵訊息

UNIT
4

關鍵訊息：

Nicole: "thank you for the extensive research you are willing to do for our company"

Robert: "The pleasure is mine. I hope I can be of service to your company."

Answer the questions.
回答問題

回答問題：

1. (B) Robert is a research consultant.
2. (B) "The pleasure is mine" means that it's Robert's pleasure to serve the company.

 Test tip

多益閱讀測驗分成單篇閱讀與多篇閱讀。單篇閱讀的解題時間應控制在每題 30～45 秒之內，把作答時間盡量留給後面的多篇閱讀。(多篇閱讀會在 Unit 8 詳細介紹。)

V. Learn by Doing

請用下方 1–5 題練習 SSA 解題技巧。

Questions 1–2 refer to the following survey.

Tutor DEF Teacher Training Series
Workshop: 4 Methods for Teaching Children English
Attendee name: *John Bradson*
Please select at least two reasons why you chose this workshop.
- ☐ My teaching skills aren't up to standard.
- ☑ I want to learn more about children's education.
- ☑ I want to make more money in this area.
- ☑ I want to know how children's cram schools are run.
- ☐ I want to **surpass** myself in English teaching.
- ☐ I just want to complete a course on this subject.

Please indicate whether or not you agree with the following statements.

	Yes	No
The speaker's instruction was easy to understand.	☐	☑
The speaker designed the workshop content to accommodate your needs.	☑	☐
The knowledge and skills I gained were useful and practical.	☑	☐

Suggestions for improvement:
Though the knowledge was useful, the speaker might need to **modify** *the way he presented the lesson content and make everything briefer.*

---

1. What is indicated about the content of the workshop?
   (A) It was about how to teach children English.
   (B) It was about how to launch a cram school.
   (C) It was on the topic of business leadership.
   (D) It was about administration.

2. What did Mr. Bradson suggest about the presenter?
   (A) He should increase his subject knowledge.
   (B) He should make the knowledge more practical.
   (C) He should present his material more briefly.
   (D) The organization of his slides should be done better.

Questions 3–5 refer to the following email.

To:	Anthony Rogerson
From:	George Frankson, Associate Manager at Engeo
Subject:	Operation of the machinery you purchased
Date:	September 27

Dear Mr. Rogerson,

I'm writing to you with reference to the machines you purchased from us last week. Firstly, we provided an operation manual for each piece of machinery. It's crucial that you follow the instructions and periodically examine the machines for damage. You can duplicate the machinery operation manual and give it to all workers in your department. If the machinery is damaged because of misuse, we will not reimburse your money. If it breaks down, please don't hesitate to notify us. We can provide help to repair it. Do not attempt to fix the machinery by yourself, as things may only get worse.

If your workers are still unsure of how to operate the machinery after studying the manual, we can **arrange** for a professional to do a basic demonstration for you. If you have any further questions about our after-sales service, please don't hesitate to leave me a message. I'll get back to you ASAP.

UNIT
4

3. What is the purpose of this email?
   (A) To provide after-sales service to a purchasing client
   (B) To promote machinery
   (C) To announce a change in a model of machinery
   (D) To place an order for some machinery

4. What should Mr. Rogerson do if the machinery breaks down?
   (A) Call another repair company
   (B) Attempt to repair the machinery by himself
   (C) Study the manual
   (D) Contact Mr. Frankson immediately

5. What is suggested about the machinery?
   (A) The way to run it is not mentioned in the manual.
   (B) It cannot be fixed if damaged.
   (C) It should be operated carefully.
   (D) It is dangerous to use.

1. **instruction** [ɪn`strʌkʃən] n. 指示說明　　

The new employee is following the **instructions** carefully to operate that complicated copy machine.

這位新員工正小心地遵循說明指南操作那臺複雜的影印機。

2. **confidential** [ˌkɑnfə`dɛnʃəl] adj. 機密的　　

We are required to lock the **confidential** files in the filing cabinet so as to protect the transaction information.

我們被要求要將機密文件鎖進檔案櫃裡，如此才能保護交易資料。

3. **extensive** [ɪk`stɛnsɪv] adj. 廣泛的；大量的　　

The office needs **extensive** alterations and renovations before we move in.

在我們搬進來之前，這間辦公室需要大規模的整修和翻新。

4. **attempt** [ə`tɛmpt] v. 試圖；嘗試　　

Do not **attempt** to ask Mr. Sanchez for a raise today. He is in a very bad mood for failing to close the deal with The Jacksons.　今天不要嘗試向 Sanchez 先生要求加薪，他因為沒有跟 Jacksons 公司談成生意而心情很糟。

5. **stack** [stæk] v. 把…疊成堆；堆放　　

Our boss asked us to **stack** up cans of Coke in the center of the store.

老闆要我們把一罐罐可樂堆疊在店中央。

6. **periodically** [ˌpɪrɪ`ɑdɪklɪ] adv. 定期地；週期性地　　

The office equipment will be tested **periodically**.　辦公室的設備會被定期測試。

7. **urgent** [`ɜ˞dʒənt] adj. 緊急的　　★★★

I need you to sign this document right now. It's very **urgent**!

我必須請你現在簽這份文件，非常緊急！

8. notify [`notə,faɪ] v. 通知

Has every employee been **notified** of the new policy on cell phone usage?

每個員工都被通知新的手機使用規定了嗎？

9. accommodation [ə,kɑmə`deʃən] n. 住處

In our company, one of the benefits for new employees is free **accommodation** at the staff dormitory for a year.

在我們公司裡，新員工的福利之一是免費住員工宿舍一年。

UNIT 4

10. reimburse [riɪm`bɝs] v. 退款；償還

The company will **reimburse** employees for the amount they have paid during their business trips.　公司會將員工在出差期間花費的金額退還。

11. duplicate [`dupləkɪt] n. 複本　v. 複製

Could you please give Ms. Butler a **duplicate** of this file? She lost its original form.

可以給 Butler 小姐一份這個檔案的複本嗎？她弄丟了原檔。

12. complete [kəm`plit] v. 完成

I **completed** the application form and mailed it this afternoon.

今天下午我已經完成申請表且寄出。

13. signature [`sɪgnətʃɚ] n. 簽名

We still need Mr. Diaz's **signature** before issuing this notification to the office.

我們還需要 Diaz 先生的簽名才會發通知給辦公室。

14. message [`mɛsɪdʒ] n. 訊息

The manager is not in this week. Would you like to leave a **message**? I'll inform him as soon as possible.　經理這個星期不在，你要留言給他嗎？我會盡快通知他。

15. correspondence [ˌkɔrəˈspɑndəns] n. 信件

Kindle Bank has moved to 6th Avenue. Please remind the secretary to send **correspondence** to its new address from now on.

Kindle 銀行已經搬到第六大道，請提醒祕書今後要將信件寄到新的地址。

---

16. informative [ɪnˈfɔrmətɪv] adj. 資訊豐富的

Check this brochure if you encounter any problems at work. It is very **informative**.

如果你遇到工作上的任何問題，查查這本小手冊，它裡面的資訊很豐富。

---

17. agreement [əˈgrimənt] n. 契約；協議

Mr. Ettinger was sued because he broke the confidentiality **agreement**.

Ettinger 先生因為違反保密協議而被告。

---

18. surpass [səˈpæs] v. 超越；優於

Ms. Long **surpasses** other employees in work performance.

Long 小姐在工作表現上優於其他員工。

---

19. modify [ˈmɑdəˌfaɪ] v. 修訂

The proposal won't be accepted unless it is **modified** thoroughly and properly.

提案不會通過，除非已被徹底且恰當地修訂過。

---

20. arrange [əˈrendʒ] v. 安排

Lisa is **arranging** her work now so that she can take two days off next week without delaying any work.

Lisa 正在安排工作進度，以便下週她能請兩天假而不會延誤任何工作。

5 A Movie Marathon

I. Warm-up Track-23

Timothy is at the Royal Theater ready to watch a musical. Right before the opening, he hears an announcement. Listen together with him, and check the boxes next to the information you get. Do not read the script while listening.

☐ How long the performance is ☐ The title of the performance

☐ How long the break during the play is ☐ The time the performance ends

☐ How many people are attending the show ☐ The time the performance begins

☐ What people can do during the intermission ☐ What people can buy in the theater

☐ What people can't do during the performance

Good evening, ladies and gentlemen. Welcome to the Royal Theater. This evening, we're very proud to present the most critically ***acclaimed*** classic musical, *Cats*, to you all. Hope you'll enjoy it. Please note that any recording of this performance, either through photographs or videos, is strictly ***prohibited***. Please turn off your cell phones for the ***duration*** of the performance. The play is in two acts with a 20–minute ***intermission*** in between. During the intermission, light refreshments will be provided in the lobby for you to purchase. A reminder that food and drinks are not allowed in the auditorium. Thank you, and we hope you have a wonderful evening.

II. Reading

Timothy is a huge fan of *Star Fancy* series. From next Monday, DMS Theater is going to have a *Star Fancy* marathon. Let's help him to decide which movies to watch.

DMS Movie Theater—
Star Fancy Series Marathon & Exhibition 16–21 August

Come to DMS Movie Theater and relive classic movies this week! Fans of *Star Fancy* series, come get **overwhelmed** by this big event!

Theater 1	Episode I *The Rise of the Empire*	Episode II *The Cost of Revolution*	Episode III *Princess Abigail*
	09:30 12:30 15:30 19:30 21:30 23:30	10:00 13:00 16:00 19:00 22:00 24:00	09:00 12:00 15:00 17:30 19:30 22:30
Theater 2	Episode IV *Clones Flow*	Episode V *Awakening of the Boys*	Episode VI *Peace*
	09:30 12:30 15:30 19:30 21:30 23:30	10:00 13:00 16:00 19:00 22:00 24:00	09:00 12:00 15:00 17:30 19:30 22:30
Theater 3	Episode I *The Rise of the Empire*	Episode II *The Cost of Revolution*	Episode III *Princess Abigail*
	10:00 13:00 16:00 19:00 22:00 24:00	09:00 12:00 15:00 17:30 19:30 22:30	09:30 12:30 15:30 19:30 21:30 23:30
Theater 4	Episode IV *Clones Flow*	Episode V *Awakening of the Boys*	Episode VI *Peace*
	10:00 13:00 16:00 19:00 22:00 24:00	09:00 12:00 15:00 17:30 19:30 22:30	09:30 12:30 15:30 19:30 21:30 23:30

※Special exhibition—Crystal **Gallery** (6F)
An **exhibition** of **collections** of movie merchandise, costumes, **statues**, and posters. Come to Exhibition Room 1 to purchase **fascinating** limited-edition products.

※Special meeting
The **producer** and **director** of the latest episode *Peace* are coming to meet all the passionate fans on August 18! Fans buying package tickets will obtain free **admission** to the meeting!

III. Tasks

A. Timothy wants to attend the special meeting. What should he do to get free admission?

☐ see episodes I to VI   ☐ buy package tickets

☐ buy merchandise of the movies   ☐ wait in line on the night of August 17

B. Below is Timothy's schedule after work. He wants to watch the film series in order, from the first episode to the sixth. Please help him complete the schedule accordingly.

Thu. 8/16	✓ *18:00–20:00 dinner with Jenny* ✓ *21:30 Theater 1, Episode I*	**Sun. 8/19**	✓ *18:00–21:00 men's night*
Fri. 8/17	✓ *17:00–21:00 work overtime* ✓ *21:30 pub date*	**Mon. 8/20**	✓ *22:00–23:00 play basketball*
Sat. 8/18		**Tue. 8/21**	

UNIT
5

IV. Test Tactics

Focus: Reading Test–Incomplete Sentences

新制多益閱讀部分的句子填空題為 30 題，每一題有一個空格，考生要從題目的四個選項中選出最適合的答案來完成句子。

題型特色：分成單字題與文法題，比例大約各半。單字題測驗字義及詞性；文法題測驗介係詞、轉折語及其他基本文法概念。

解題關鍵： 1.強化單字力與基礎文法概念。 2.判斷空格所需詞性。

以下方試題為例：

1. I'd like to show my _____ to all the staff who helped prepare for our year-end party.

    (A) commission

    (B) confidence

    (C) awareness

    (D) appreciation

➡ 單字題，測驗字義，各選項字義為 (A) 傭金 (B) 信心 (C) 意識 (D) 感激，故選 (D)。

2. The **enrollment** in the business seminar will _____ an arm and a leg.

(A) **cost**

(B) costed

(C) costs

(D) costly

> 單字題，測驗詞性，助動詞後需接原形動詞，故選 (A)。

3. The electronic company's new entertainment system _____ be rolled out next year.

(A) will

(B) was

(C) have

(D) did

> 文法題，出現未來時間點，需用未來式，故選 (A)。

V. Learn by Doing

現在請完成以下題目，找出自己最需要加強的環節是單字力、詞性判斷能力還是文法概念。

1. The auto parts exhibition _____ been put off until next Wednesday.

(A) was

(B) will

(C) has

(D) are

2. The movie was a box office hit even though the **critics** gave it bad _____.

(A) **reviews**

(B) reviewed

(C) reviewer

(D) reviewing

3. Isaac found the magazine quite fascinating, _____ he decided to **subscribe** to it.

(A) so

(B) although

(C) but

(D) then

4. The employees are _____ by managers to keep a daily record of their work progress.

(A) specified

(B) required

(C) challenged

(D) questioned

5. The **novice** movie director is so talented that she _____ been awarded twice.

(A) has

(B) was

(C) will

(D) had

6. The general manager already has a _____ of contracts he signed with other companies this year.

(A) collect

(B) collecting

(C) collected

(D) collection

7. The workers need to keep a record of the number of goods in stock and make sure we are not _____ low on any supplies.

(A) going

(B) running

(C) growing

(D) making

8. _____ the stress he is under at work can be rather overwhelming at times, he is still able to cope with it.

(A) As

(B) Although

(C) Despite

(D) Whether

9. The data released _____ to the current records on our company's financial situation.

(A) corresponds

(B) correspondence

(C) corresponding

(D) correspondent

UNIT
5

 Test tip

詞類變化題亦測驗考生對字尾意義的掌握，如字尾 -ment、-tion、-ence 多為名詞。

VI. Vocabulary

1. **entertainment** [ˌɛntəˈtenmənt] n. 娛樂 ★★★

The study indicates that on average, American teenagers spend about $100 per month on their personal **entertainment**.

研究顯示美國青少年每個月平均花費一百美元在個人娛樂上。

2. **acclaimed** [əˈklemd] adj. 受到讚揚的 ★★★

Phantom of the Opera is a critically **acclaimed** play.

《歌劇魅影》是一齣受評論家所讚譽的戲劇。

3. **prohibit** [proˈhɪbɪt] v. 禁止 ★★★

The use of cell phones is **prohibited** during the show. 演出期間禁止使用手機。

4. **duration** [djuˈreʃən] n. 期間 ★★★

The audience kept laughing for the **duration** of the movie.

觀眾在電影播放期間一直放聲大笑。

5. **intermission** [ˌɪntəˈmɪʃən] n. 中場休息 ★★★

Let's get some refreshments in the hall during the **intermission**.

中場休息的時候，我們去大廳吃些點心吧！

6. **overwhelm** [ˌovəˈhwɛlm] v. 征服；使情緒激動 ★★★

Jill got **overwhelmed** when listening to the orchestra playing her favorite symphony.

聽到管弦樂團演奏最喜愛的交響樂曲令 Jill 激動不已。

7. **gallery** [ˈgælərɪ] n. 陳列室；畫廊 ★★★

Here is an invitation to the exhibition at the National Contemporary **Gallery**.

這裡有一張當代國家藝廊展覽的邀請函。

8. **exhibition** [ˌɛksə`bɪʃən] n. 展覽

There is a new **exhibition** of the works of the outstanding painter, Meirion Ginsberg, at Matt's Gallery.　Matt's 藝廊有傑出畫家 Meirion Ginsberg 的畫作新展覽。

9. **collection** [kə`lɛkʃən] n. 收藏品；一批物品

Fedrick bought another painting at an auction to add to his private art **collection**.
Fedrick 在拍賣會上買了另一幅畫，替他私人藝術收藏品又添一筆。

10. **statue** [`stætʃu] n. 雕像

They plan to put up a **statue** of the mascot right in front of the gate of the amusement park.　他們計劃把吉祥物的雕像設置在遊樂場的大門前。

UNIT
5

11. **fascinating** [`fæsṇetɪŋ] adj. 吸引人的；極好的

Did you see the Van Gogh exhibition? All the works were **fascinating**!
你看了這次的梵谷畫展嗎？所有作品都非常好看！

12. **producer** [prə`dusɚ] n. 製作人

A TV **producer** needs to oversee a project from conception to completion.
從概念發想到方案執行完成，電視製作人都需要全程監控。

13. **director** [də`rɛktɚ] n. 導演

It is said that the **director** missed his own movie's premiere because of the quarrel with the leading actor.　據傳導演和男主角發生爭執，所以在首映會中缺席。

14. **admission** [əd`mɪʃən] n. 准許入場，准許進入

How much do they charge for **admission** to the sculpture exhibition?
雕塑展的入場費用為多少？

15. enrollment [ɪnˋrolmənt] n. 登記；註冊

The **enrollment** fee for the music class is quite reasonable and affordable.

這門音樂課程的註冊費相當合理也負擔得起。

---

16. cost [kɔst] v. 花費

The musical tickets we booked **cost** $55 each.

我們訂的音樂會入場券一張五十五元。

---

17. critic [ˋkrɪtɪk] n. 評論家

Being a film **critic**, Aurora watches many films in different genres every day.

身為影評，Aurora 每天都看許多部不同種類的電影。

---

18. review [rɪˋvju] n. 評論

Director George Miller's latest film got excellent **reviews** from almost all the movie critics.　George Miller 導演的最新電影幾乎得到所有影評們的一致好評。

---

19. subscribe [səbˋskraɪb] v. 訂閱

It is a good time to **subscribe** to *Science Up* magazine, for it has a discount up to 60 % off now.　這是一個訂閱《Science Up》雜誌的好時機，因為現在有四折優惠。

---

20. novice [ˋnɑvɪs] n. 新手；初學者

Maggie is a theater **novice**. She just started watching plays and musicals recently.

Maggie 是劇場新手，她近來才開始看戲劇和音樂劇。

6 Work Schedule Arrangement

I. Warm-up Track-26

Mr. Newton's secretary would like to inform him of some changes to his work arrangement. Please listen to the secretary's phone message and help Mr. Newton update his calendar. Do not read the script while listening.

Wed.	Thu.	Fri.
9:00 a.m. visit to GoodBaby Food 12:00 p.m. lunch with Mrs. Coco Melzer		8:00 a.m. weekly meeting
7:30 p.m. dinner with family at Italian Mama	~~2:00 p.m. meeting with Mr. Donald~~ go to the baseball game	1:00 p.m. meeting at BodyCare Food Building A, Room 305

Morning, boss! Ms. Gibson from BodyCare Food called early this morning to inform you of the changes to this Friday's meeting. The meeting will take place at 10:00 a.m. instead of 1:00 p.m. The venue also changed from the Conference Room 305 to 308 at BodyCare Food Building A. Also, I rescheduled your meeting with Mr. Donald at 2:00 p.m. this Thursday for 2:00 p.m. this Friday. In that way, you will have a whole day off on Thursday. You can then go to your son's baseball game that afternoon. If you have any problems with those changes I made, just call me on my mobile phone.

II. Reading

Elmore's company, Global Enterprise, is going to move its headquarters to somewhere bigger. Elmore is chatting with Alvin, who works in another company located in the same building.

> **Alvin:** I've heard you are about to move to bigger offices.
>
> **Elmore:** That's right. We've hired quite a lot of new staff members. Global Enterprise is growing fast.
>
> **Alvin:** Indeed it is. I think it will soon become one of the leading companies in the world!
>
> **Elmore:** I hope so! We're all happy about the **achievement** we've made. See this medal of honor? I got this last Friday at our company's annual **awards ceremony**.
>
> **Alvin:** Congratulations! That means your manager has a positive **appraisal** of your **dedication** to the company!
>
> **Elmore:** Well, I worked so hard for every **assignment** I got because I had one goal in mind.
>
> **Alvin:** What's that?
>
> **Elmore:** The **incentive** payments for the winner of this medal of honor!

A month later at the Aroma Café, Elmore bumped into Alvin.

> **Elmore:** Hey, Alvin.
>
> **Alvin:** Hi, Elmore! How's everything going?
>
> **Elmore:** I just finished **evaluating** the work **performance** of the new employees. Though some of them are **inexperienced**, they are really hard-working. How about you? Is everything OK?
>
> **Alvin:** Well, one of our managers turned in his **resignation** and left the company all of a sudden. We're shocked and busy handling the work he left behind.
>
> **Elmore:** Sorry to hear that. Is that the reason why you look so exhausted?
>
> **Alvin:** Not exactly. I've been having a serious toothache these days. I've got to go now, or I'll be late for my dentist **appointment**.
>
> **Elmore:** Take care! Bye.

III. Tasks

A. Please answer the questions below.

1. Why is Elmore moving to bigger offices?

_____

2. What did Elmore get in return for his hard work?

_____

3. Why is Elmore working so hard?

_____

4. What has Alvin been busy doing?

_____

5. Why is Alvin so exhausted?

_____

B. Role-play the dialogue with your partner twice and volunteer to present it in front of the class!

UNIT
6

IV. Test Tactics

Focus: Listening Test—Short Talks

多益聽力部分的短講題有 10 個題組，每題組有 3 題。每段短講皆僅播放一次。

題型特色： 1. 如同多益對話題，題目與選項皆印於紙本。

2. 每題組皆為獨白，訊息量大於對話題。

解題關鍵：如同對話題 (見 Unit 2)，預先速讀題目以在聆聽短講時掌握關鍵訊息。

以下方試題為例：

1. Who are most likely the listeners?

   (A) Computer engineers

   (B) Customer service staff

   (C) Real estate investors

   (D) Corporate lawyers

2. What are they planning to establish in Manila?

   (A) A film studio

   (B) A construction company

   (C) A law firm

   (D) A manufacturing factory

3. Who will resign from the company?

   (A) The assistant manager

   (B) The marketing department manager

   (C) The vice president

   (D) The associate general manager

在短講播放以前，速讀題目時應掌握問題關鍵：

題目關鍵字	聽力要點
listeners: engineers, customer service staff, investors, or lawyers ➡	聽出說話對象是工程師、客服人員、投資者還是律師
establish in Manila ➡	細節一：關於在 Manila 建立什麼
Who will resign ➡	細節二：關於誰要辭職

現在請根據上述聽力要點來聆聽這則短講，請試著一邊聆聽，一邊作答。 Track-27

剛剛在聆聽過程中，根據聽力要點所掌握的關鍵訊息：

聽力要點	關鍵訊息
聽出說話對象是工程師、客服人員、投資者還是律師 ➡	(1) introducing our future business plans and projects (2) We will certainly get a high return on this investment.
細節一：關於在 Manila 建立什麼 ➡	set up a construction company in Manila
細節二：關於誰要辭職 ➡	the resignation of our assistant manager

因此正確答案為： 1. ___C___ 2. ___B___ 3. ___A___

如果覺得有點困難，可以翻開解析本的聽力腳本，搭配腳本再多聽幾次。

現在請練習第 4–9 題 (共兩題組)。先速讀題目，寫下題目關鍵字，再聆聽短講，聽寫完成關鍵訊息，最後作答。 **Track**-28

4. Which department does the speaker work at?

   (A) The manufacturing department

   (B) The retail department

   (C) The sales department

   (D) The administration department

5. What problem does the speaker talk about?

   (A) The workers are too lazy.

   (B) Too many items were delivered.

   (C) They received fewer parts than they ordered.

   (D) Their machinery fails to work properly.

6. What delay will happen because of this problem?

   (A) A delay in production

   (B) A delay in sales

   (C) A delay in processing of paperwork

   (D) A delay in receiving emails

UNIT
6

題目關鍵字	關鍵訊息
_____ ⇒	This is Ryan calling from the _____ department.
_____ ⇒	There are _____ in the boxes than we ordered, which will cause a delay in _____.
_____	

Answers　4. _____　5. _____　6. _____

7. What is the purpose of this talk?

   (A) To promote a product

   (B) To introduce a guest speaker

   (C) To call for investment in real estate

   (D) To announce a reward

8. What field is George Canny expert at?

   (A) Economics

   (B) Marketing

   (C) Education

   (D) Real estate

9. What is Mr. Canny's speech about?

   (A) How and when to invest in international real estate

   (B) When to invest in the stock market

   (C) How to become a stockbroker

   (D) How to sell cars

 Test tip

短講題組的三題題目中，第一題不一定問細節，也有可能問內容的整體概念，例如短講主題、說話目的、說話對象、說話場合。面對這類型題目時的解題技巧有三：

1. 速讀時看完四個選項。
2. 特別注意聽短講的第一句話 (topic sentence)。
3. 用所聽到的細節推測主旨。例如聽到 strawberry、watermelon、lemon 等字眼，則可推知主旨應與水果有關。

題目關鍵字	關鍵訊息
_____	➡ George Canny, our _____, started his career as a real estate investor right here in Cambodia.
_____	➡ expertise in the field of _____ development and investment
_____	➡ talk on the topic of how and when to _____ _____

Answers 7._____ 8._____ 9._____

V. Learn by Doing

請完成下列兩題組，訓練自己預先速讀題目以掌握聽力關鍵訊息的能力。 Track-29

1. Where does the speaker most likely work?

   (A) A drugstore

   (B) An auto parts shop

   (C) A furniture factory

   (D) A hospital

2. What problem does the speaker mention?

   (A) The drugs are sold out.

   (B) The auto parts don't fit the car.

   (C) The gearbox is not in stock.

   (D) Mr. Usher will have to wait another month.

3. What does Rocket instruct the listener to do?

   (A) Come to the shop to pay the bill

   (B) Wait another week for the repairs

   (C) Go to another shop

   (D) Buy a different gearbox

4. What event is being announced?

   (A) A blood donation activity

   (B) A badminton tournament

   (C) A carnival

   (D) A concert

5. When will the event take place?

   (A) June 17th and 18th

   (B) July 17th and 18th

   (C) June 18th and 19th

   (D) July 18th and 19th

6. Where will the event be held?

   (A) TPC community

   (B) Lillian's Club

   (C) The city hall

   (D) The blood center

UNIT 6

7. What is the purpose of this meeting?

   (A) To keep in touch with the president's goals

   (B) To discuss how to increase sales

   (C) To update the network platform

   (D) To brainstorm new business ideas

8. Where is the company planning to open new stores?

   (A) In Sydney

   (B) In Melbourne

   (C) In the north

   (D) In the west

9. What does the speaker say about the platform?

(A) It has brought a rise in sales.

(B) It provides access to the Internet.

(C) It can analyze marketing data.

(D) It will help employees get information.

VI. Vocabulary Track-30–31

1. **achievement** [ə`tʃivmənt] n. 成就

Getting this contract signed would be a real **achievement**.

簽定這份合約會是大功一件。

2. **awards ceremony** [ə`wɔrds `sɛrəmonɪ] n. 頒獎典禮

The CEO honored outstanding employees of the year at the annual **awards ceremony**.　CEO 在年度頒獎典禮上表揚當年度傑出員工。

3. **appraisal** [ə`prezl̩] n. 評價；評估

The company will hold its annual job **appraisals** next week.

下星期公司將進行年度的工作表現評估。

4. **dedication** [ˌdɛdə`keʃən] n. 貢獻

The general manager proposed a toast and thanked the staff for their **dedication**.

總經理舉杯敬酒，感謝員工們的貢獻。

5. **assignment** [ə`saɪnmənt] n. 工作；作業 ★★★

Oliver has applied for a two-year **assignment** to the Singapore office.

Oliver 申請了為期兩年駐派在新加坡的工作。

6. incentive [ɪnˈsɛntɪv] n. 激勵

The reward system provides an **incentive** for employees to work harder.

這個獎勵系統能激勵員工更加努力工作。

7. evaluate [ɪˈvæljuˌet] v. 評定；估價

The waiters in this restaurant are **evaluated** annually for their meal service.

這間餐廳的服務生每年接受餐點服務水準的評等。

8. performance [pɚˈfɔrməns] n. 表現

The company intends to improve its financial **performance** and expand its business. 公司企圖改善財務表現並擴大企業規模。

9. inexperienced [ɪnɪkˈspɪrɪənst] adj. 經驗不足的；不熟練的

One of the good traditions in our office is that senior employees coach **inexperienced** ones. 我們公司的優良傳統之一是資深員工會培訓經驗不足的員工。

10. resignation [ˌrɛzɪgˈneʃən] n. 辭呈；辭職

It is said that Roger handed in his **resignation** this morning, but the boss refused to accept it. 據聞 Roger 今天早上交出辭呈，但老闆拒絕接受。

11. appointment [əˈpɔɪntmənt] n. 任命；會面

The secretary just called to ask if she could postpone the **appointment** with you to 4 p.m. 祕書剛才來電詢問可否將與您的會面延後至下午四點。

12. real estate [ˈrɪəl əstet] n. 房地產

Muhammad invested in **real estate** and received a good return on the investment.

Muhammad 投資房地產並得到優渥的投資報酬。

13. independently [ˌɪndɪˈpɛndəntli] adv. 獨立地

Luiz works **independently** and always finishes his projects on his own.

Luiz 在工作上很獨立，總是獨立完成企劃。

UNIT
6

14. contribution [ˌkɑntrəˈbjuʃən] n. 貢獻

Joseph's **contribution** to this company was to establish complete personnel policies.　Joseph 對公司的貢獻是制定了完整的人事政策。

15. successor [səkˈsɛsɚ] n. 繼任者

The company is seeking a **successor** to its managing supervisor. That position has been vacant for three months.

公司正在尋覓常務監事的繼任者，這個職位已經懸缺三個月。

16. appreciate [əˈpriʃɪˌet] v. 感謝

In the awards ceremony, John especially **appreciated** the advice that his boss and colleagues once gave him.

頒獎典禮上，John 特別感謝老闆和同事曾經給他的建議。

17. transfer [trænsˈfɝ] v. 調職；遷移

Joel was **transferred** to the headquarters from a local branch after just half a year.

Joel 僅僅在半年內就從地方分部被調職至總部。

18. expertise [ˌɛkspɚˈtiz] n. 專精；專長

Savannah is known for her **expertise** in developing marketing strategies.

Savannah 以其開發市場策略的專長聞名。

19. authority [əˈθɔrətɪ] n. 權力；權限

We will give our lawyers **authority** to speak and make decisions on our behalf.

我們將授權律師代表我們發言和做決定。

20. eligible [ˈɛlɪdʒəbl] adj. 適用的；合格的 ★★★

Eli called the personnel department and inquired if he was **eligible** for early retirement.　Eli 致電人事部門詢問他是否符合提早退休的條件。

7 A Trip to Greece

● **Setting:** Travel ● **Focus:** Reading Test—Text Completion

I. Warm-up

Mr. and Mrs. Ortiz are planning to visit Greece. They just got an email from the **travel agency**. Please read the email and take a note for them!

✉
To : Mr. Owen Ortiz, Mrs. Olivia Ortiz
From : Ruth Haley, Travel With Me Travel
Date : January 25th
Subject : The travel arrangements for your trip to Greece
Attachments: 📎 *Itinerary*

Dear Mr. & Mrs. Ortiz,

Thank you for traveling with TWM Travel. This email is to **confirm** that we have made the following arrangements for your trip to Greece. Please see the attached itinerary.

Your flight leaves at 7:45 a.m., on January 31st. Please arrive at the airport at least two hours ahead of time. Our representative—the tour leader, Rocky Wu— will be waiting for you at the **departure** hall of **Terminal** 1 at 5:30 a.m. He will give you your **boarding passes** after confirming your identities.

Your expected **arrival** time in Greece is January 31st at 7:45 p.m. The **approximate** flight time is 12 hours. Rocky will then take you by bus to your hotel.

Please contact us if you have any questions. We wish you a pleasant trip!

Ruth Haley

NOTE

1. Time to arrive at the airport: _____

2. Meeting the tour leader _____ at _____ .

3. Flight leaves at _____ and arrives in Greece at _____

4. Flight time is about _____ .

II. Reading

Mr. and Mrs. Ortiz finally arrived in Greece and checked in to the hotel. After they entered their hotel room, they found a welcome card on a table.

Caesar's Hotel

1 ☐

2 ☐ We are honored to receive you in our hotel. We hope your stay here is the most pleasant and that your **accommodations** are as nice as you expect. Please be assured that we are ready to **assist** you at any time throughout your stay.

The hotel is located near Athens city center. Buses 16, 21, 258, and 655 stop 3 ☐ outside the hotel and go to the city center every 15-25 minutes. If you would 4 ☐ like to take a taxi into the city center, make a restaurant reservation, or order tickets to plays or movies, please contact the **front desk**, and we will be happy to help you.

Available **amenities** and **facilities** offered in Caesar's Hotel include a 5 ☐ swimming pool, a tennis court, fitness centers, vending machines, lounge bars, restaurants, etc. You're welcome to use them.

If you have any questions, please don't hesitate to contact us. We wish you a memorable visit to Greece and hope to have many opportunities to serve you in the future.

Michael Porter 6 ☐

Hotel Manager

III. Tasks

There is so much information on the welcome card. Please work with your partner to sort out the information and write (A) to (F) in the blanks.

(A) Hotel amenities

(B) Nearby traffic information

(C) Hotel name

(D) Hotel manager

(E) Counter service

(F) Greetings

IV. Test Tactics

Focus: Reading Test—Text Completion

多益閱讀部分的段落填空共四個題組，每題組有四題。

題型特色：類似於克漏字題型，但空格內可能填入單字、片語或完整句子。

解題關鍵：僅閱讀必要資訊以快速解題，把時間留給後方較為耗時的閱讀測驗。

以下方試題為例：

Questions 1 to 4 refer to the following notice.

UNIT
7

Are you searching for a five star hotel with a great reputation for high quality customer service? Peace Hotel is the place for you. If you are traveling in our *picturesque* city and want to see wonderful ------- during the day and enjoy high
1.
class accommodations at night, we offer you good value ------- money. If you don't
2.
want to miss any of the famous tourist attractions in our city, don't worry! ------- For
3.
more information, please visit our website. You can make a reservation with us by
------- 1234 4321 or by visiting our local travel agency.
4.

作答時只需要閱讀前後文必要資訊。

1. (A) environment
   (B) setting
   (C) scenery
   (D) condition

➡ . . . you are traveling in our beautiful city and want to see wonderful _____ during the day. . . . 此為單字題，各選項字義為 (A) 環境 (B) 背景 (C) 風景 (D) 條件，故選 (C)。

2. (A) for
   (B) with
   (C) of
   (D) to

➡ . . . we offer you good value _____ money. 此為文法片語題，value for money 是固定用法，意指價格划算的東西，故選 (A)。

3. (A) We offer high quality room service.
   (B) We are one of the most famous hotels.
   (C) They are always full of tourists in the spring.
   (D) They are all easily *accessible* from our hotel.

➡ 此為完整句子題， 前文是 If you don't want to miss any of the famous tourist attractions in our city, don't worry! 故後文應提及為何旅客不必擔心會錯過著名景點，答案為 (D)，這些景點從飯店出發都很容易到達。

4. (A) call
   (B) calling
   (C) calls
   (D) called

➡ . . . by _____ 1234 4321 or by visiting. . . . 此為詞類變化題，介係詞後需接名詞，此處需要動名詞，故選 (B)。

V. Learn by Doing

請閱讀必要資訊，快速判別答案，完成以下 1–8 題。

Questions 1–4 refer to the following article.

Brooklyn Airlines is in hot water once again. Today, a video clip of an argument between two **flight attendants** and a passenger is going viral on the Internet. Apparently, the flight was -------. The number of passengers who checked in
1.
exceeded the number of seats -------. The **airline** issued an apology to all
2.
passengers for what happened on the plane. All passengers were offered a voucher valid for any future flight with the airline. -------, many passengers expressed
3.
dissatisfaction as the vouchers expire within six months. -------.
4.

1. (A) overbook

   (B) overbooks

   (C) overbooked

   (D) overbooking

2. (A) free

   (B) occupied

   (C) useful

   (D) available

3. (A) However

   (B) Specifically

   (C) Otherwise

   (D) Additionally

4. (A) Each passenger should get a voucher.

   (B) The video clip can become more popular.

   (C) They think there should be more empty seats.

   (D) Many do not have plans to travel that soon.

UNIT
7

Questions 5–8 refer to the following email.

To: Allison von Franck
From: booking13@happytravel.com
Date: Oct. 22
Subject: Flight and hotel
Attachments: Itinerary; Hotel description

Dear Ms. Franck,

Thank you for your *inquiry* about the *airfare* and accommodations. The *round-trip* airfare will be $1,342. Please check the attached flight itinerary to make sure it suits your needs and schedule. ------- hotels, there are many types that are available,
5.
depending on if you want to be in the city, on the beach or closer to the mountains.

------- Take your time to make the decision that best suits your ------- vacation.
6.   7.

Please get back to us at your earliest convenience so we can make all of the -------
8.
for you. If you have any questions, please send me an email. We are pleased to be of service.

5. (A) Despite
   (B) As for
   (C) Due to
   (D) Among

6. (A) Please see the second attached file.
   (B) We have information on local restaurants.
   (C) You should choose a beach resort.
   (D) Why don't you try a mountain cottage?

7. (A) desire
   (B) desired
   (C) desiring
   (D) desires

8. (A) tours
   (B) amenities
   (C) reservations
   (D) designs

VI. Vocabulary Track -32-33

1. **travel agency** [`trævl̩ edʒənsɪ] n. 旅行社

   The **travel agency** will inform us of the time and place to gather.

   旅行社會通知我們集合的時間和地點。

2. **itinerary** [aɪ`tɪnəˌrɛrɪ] n. 行程

   Your **itinerary** has been well arranged by the travel agency.

   你的行程已由旅行社安排妥當。

3. **confirm** [kən`fɝm] v. 確認；確定

   Hotel bookings will be **confirmed** through phone calls two days before check-in.

   旅館預約會在入住兩天前以電話確認。

4. **departure** [dɪ`pɑrtʃɚ] n. 離開；啟程

   Their **departure** was delayed due to aircraft mechanical problems.

   他們的出發時間由於飛機機械故障而延誤。

5. **terminal** [`tɝmənl̩] n. 航站

   The second floor of **Terminal** 1 is for domestic departures.

   第一航站的二樓是國內線離境。

6. **boarding pass** [`bordɪŋ pæs] n. 登機證

   Without a **boarding pass**, you won't have permission to board.

   沒有登機證，你就不會得到登機許可。

7. **arrival** [ə`raɪvl̩] n. 抵達，到達 ★★★

   Williams heard the loudspeaker announce the late **arrival** of his flight.

   Williams 聽到廣播宣布他的班機誤點。

UNIT
7

8. approximate [ə`prɑksəmət] adj. 大約

The **approximate** cost of this round-the-world trip is $25,000.

這趟環遊世界之旅大約花費兩萬五千美元。

9. accommodations [ə,kɑmə`deʃənz] n. 住宿服務

This hostel provides backpackers with inexpensive **accommodations**.

這間旅舍提供背包客便宜的住宿。

10. assist [ə`sɪst] v. 幫助

If you encounter any problems, just phone the front desk and our staff will **assist** you. 無論您遇到任何問題都可以打電話至櫃臺，我們的工作人員將協助處理。

11. front desk [`frʌnt dɛsk] n. 櫃臺

Visitors are gathering in the hotel lobby, waiting to check in at the **front desk**.

遊客們聚集在飯店大廳，等著在櫃臺辦入住手續。

12. amenity [ə`mɛnətɪ] n. 設施

The King Resort is famous for its luxurious **amenities**, such as a large swimming pool, shopping center, and movie library.

King 渡假中心以豪華設施聞名，例如大型的游泳池、購物中心和電影館。

13. facilities [fə`sɪlətɪz] n. 設施

After the expansion, the hotel will offer not only sports **facilities** but also medical and shopping ones. 擴建之後，旅館不但會提供運動設施，也會有醫療和購物設施。

14. picturesque [ˌpɪktʃə`rɛsk] adj. 如畫般美麗的

Benjamin likes to take a walk along the **picturesque** street.

Benjamin 喜歡沿著這條如畫般美麗的街道散步。

15. accessible [æk`sɛsəbl] adj. 可到達的；可得到的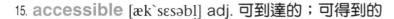

One of the biggest reasons why this historical site attracts so many tourists is that it is **accessible** by mass transit.

此歷史景點之所以吸引大量觀光客，原因之一是搭乘大眾運輸就可到達。

16. flight attendant [`flaɪt ətɛndənt] n. 空服人員

The service provided by the **flight attendants** is thoughtful and considerate.

空服員所提供的服務非常細心和周到。

17. airline [`ɛrlaɪn] n. 航空公司

Many **airlines** nowadays use electronic ticketing to reduce costs.

現今許多航空公司使用電子機票以減少成本。

18. inquiry [ɪn`kwaɪəri] n. 詢問

The travel agency received a lot of **inquiries** about the package tour.

旅行社接到許多對於此套裝行程的詢問。

19. airfare [`ɛrfɛr] n. 機票票價

The **airfares** are going to increase by at least 15% next month.

機票票價下個月至少漲價百分之十五。

UNIT
7

20. round-trip [`raʊnd͵trɪp] adj. 來回的

The cost of **round-trip** tickets is 10% cheaper than two one-way tickets.

來回票的價格比兩張單程票便宜百分之十。

8 An Expanding Manufacturing Company

I. Warm-up Track-34

Mr. Webb wants to call Ms. Rodgers, but he found her business card was stained with ink. Listen to the voicemail, and help Mr. Webb find out the right number he should press. Do not read the script while listening.

Humphreys Manufacturing Corporation

HUMPHREYS

Sales Department Manager
Janet Rodgers

🏠 67 A. Mabini Street, Caloocan, Philippines
📞 TEL: (office) +63 (2) 775 9990 #   📱 +63 0905
✉ email: janetrg821@hump
@ website: humphreysmanu

Mr. Webb should press _____ to reach Ms. Rodgers.

Welcome to Humphreys Manufacturing Corporation. Thank you for calling us. We are sorry that all our representatives are **currently** busy. Please hold. We will take your call as soon as possible. If you know your **party**'s **extension** number, please dial it now. For Management, please press 1. For Accounting, please press 2. For Personnel, please press 3. For Warehousing, please press 4. For Sales, please press 5. For Marketing, please press 6. To speak with the operator, please press 0 or stay on the line. For your information, our office hours are Monday through Friday, 9 a.m. to 6 p.m. Thank you for calling and have a nice day.

II. Reading

Please read the following news.

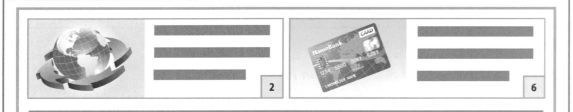

Local Daily News

Metalix Metal Company Expands Its Kingdom

Metalix Metal Company (MMC), one of the largest and *state-of-the-art* metal companies in the U.S., opened its 8th plant this Monday in Pennsylvania.

MMC has a unique marketing network and *supplies* more than 80 customers in 16 countries. Its quick expansion does not surprise market analysts, for they have long *predicted* its likely growth since it was first established in 2006.

MMC has taken out a few *patents* on their new products recently. The CEO Lee Welch said in an interview this Monday, "We are always trying to develop new products and improve our existing ones. It is our passion for understanding and meeting our clients' needs that has been driving us to innovate."

MMC has won many awards in metal product design competitions. They always *utilize* the latest technology, and all their products are made in an eco-friendly way. "The *application* of new technology has helped us reduce the use of water and *electricity*, and the pollution as well," said Lee Welch.

The opening of the new plant annoyed some residents of Pennsylvania. They didn't want to live so near a factory. Nevertheless, the *majority* of residents welcome the factory's arrival, for it has brought hundreds of jobs for the locals.

UNIT
8

III. Tasks

Please form groups of three. Discuss with your group members and list the main points of the news.

What I learned from the news:
1. *MMC opened its 8th plant this Monday in Pennsylvania.*
2. _____
3. _____
4. _____
5. _____

IV. Test Tactics

Focus: Reading Test—Multiple Passage Reading

多益閱讀部分的多篇閱讀是難度最高的題型，亦是取得高分的關鍵。此部分共五個題組，每題組五題。前兩個題組各有兩篇文章，後三個題組各有三篇文章。

題型特色：除了詢問文章大意及細節的典型閱測題型 (見 Unit 4)，也可能出現需要「連結資訊」才能作答的題目。

解題關鍵：採用 SSA 解題步驟 (Skim the questions. → Scan the text. → Answer the questions.) 快速作答，並針對「資訊連結題」整合所需關鍵資訊。

以下方試題為例：

Questions 1-5 refer to the following emails.

From: bturner@coldmail.com
To: fchazel@kmail.com
Date: June 14
Subject: Setting up a factory in China
Dear Ms. Chen, This is Bob Turner. As general manager of Winner Industries, I am writing to you to explain our plan to expand our business enterprise into China. As you understand the

local market and the best way to set up a factory in China, I hope we can collaborate on the task of being profitable in the Chinese market. Once our work permit application has been accepted, we will build an auto parts factory and a **warehouse** of vast **dimensions** in Northeast China. Can you recommend which place in Northeast China we should choose?

Also, we are increasing our manufacturing **capability**. We plan to utilize state-of-the-art, energy-efficient machinery, but we find that some of the machines are quite **complicated** to use. We would like to have your professionals demonstrate how to operate them.

We expect that the process of setting up this factory will last about four months. Please let me know what you think and give me advice on how to do better at setting up the factory.

Thank you.
Bob Turner

| **From:** fchazel@kmail.com |
| **To:** bturner@coldmail.com |
| **Date:** June 15 |
| **Subject:** Re: Setting up a factory in China |

Dear Mr. Turner,

Thanks for your email regarding your business plan. I feel that many of your ideas are correct and quite realistic. It's wise to invest in the right machinery so that you will be able to reduce costs and make more profit.

I suggest you shorten the factory set-up time to two and a half months, and we will be able to get ahead of the local competition. When everything is ready, I will send some professionals to carry out an **inspection** of your machinery and give the demonstration. As for where to build the factory and the warehouse, I recommend Shenyang, since the local government adopts **preferential** policies for foreign companies.

I sincerely hope that we can create a **mutually** beneficial relationship in the near future.

Best regards,
Fang Chen

UNIT
8

1. Why did Mr. Turner write his email?

   (A) To apologize

   (B) To ask for advice

   (C) To give suggestions

   (D) To advertise job opportunities

2. When will Winner Industries set up their factory?

   (A) After they find more customers

   (B) After they receive the work permit

   (C) Before they finish moving

   (D) Before they build the warehouse

3. Where is Winner Industries planning to set up the factory?

   (A) Southwest China

   (B) Southeast China

   (C) Northwest China

   (D) Northeast China

4. What does Ms. Chen mean when she writes "the right machinery" on line 2 in her email?

   (A) Machines that can be used for a good purpose

   (B) Machines that are advanced and power saving

   (C) Machines that will be equipped in a proper way

   (D) Machines that are massive and complicated

5. Why does Ms. Chen suggest Mr. Turner shorten the time to set up his factory?

   (A) To get ahead of their competitors

   (B) To move before policies change

   (C) To save more time and money

   (D) To purchase cheaper machines

解題步驟如下表：

Skim the questions.	Scan the text.	Answer the questions.
1. Mr. Turner 為何寫信？	寫信目的通常可見於信首或信末 ▼ Please let me know what you think and give me advice. . . . (第一篇倒數第一至二行)	(B) To ask for advice
2. 何時設廠？	Once our work permit application has been accepted, we will build an auto parts factory. . . . (第一篇第四至五行)	(B) After they receive the work permit
3. 何處設廠？	. . . we will build an auto parts factory . . . in Northeast China. (第一篇第五至六行)	(D) Northeast China
4. "the right machinery" 是指什麼？	*資訊連結題 I feel that many of your ideas are correct and quite realistic. It's wise to invest in the right machinery. . . . (第二篇第一至二行) ▼ 從 "your ideas" 可知線索應在第一篇提到 machinery 的地方 ▼ . . . plan to utilize state-of-the-art, energy-efficient machinery. . . . (第一篇第八至九行)	(B) Machines that are advanced and power saving

UNIT
8

| 5. Ms. Chen 建議縮短時間的原因？ | I suggest you shorten the factory set-up time to two and a half months, and we will be able to get ahead of the local competition. (第二篇第四至五行) | (A) To get ahead of their competitors |

V. Learn by Doing

請用下方 1-5 題練習資訊連結以及 SSA 解題技巧。

Questions 1-5 refer to the following advertisement, information board, and email.

GLOBAL GYM HOLIDAY SPECIAL

Make getting fit your New Year's Resolution.

We are here to help!

From now until New Year's Eve, Global Gym is holding a special on all gym memberships. For current members, all memberships of one year or longer will be 20% off. And for any new member you introduce, we offer a 30% discount!

Join us on New Year's Eve as we will have our annual New Year's Eve celebration. All our facilities will be available for all members, including new members whose memberships begin on January 1st. Doors will open at 6 p.m. and the party will last until 4 a.m.

All our personal trainers will be on hand for complimentary consultations on both New Year's Eve and the first week of the New Year, regardless of membership levels.

Global Gym Membership

Term	Fitness	Pool	Personal Trainers
*1 month	$35	$10	$15
3 months	$85	$25	$35
6 months	$150	$40	$60
12 months	$250	$65	$100
2 years	$400	$110	$160
3 years	$550	$140	$200
5 years	$800	$200	$310

*1 month memberships limited to first-time members

To: servicedesk@globalgym.com	
From: jsekelow@kmail.com	
Date: December 17	
Subject: About New Year special	

I'm already a member of Global Gym, and my girlfriend would like to become one. I'm going to purchase two memberships, one for myself, the other as a Christmas present for my girlfriend. Seeing your advertisement, I'm glad to know that I can get free consultations as well as good discounts on both our memberships. But the new membership will not take effect until January 1st. I would like to know if my girlfriend will be able to attend the New Year's Eve party from 6 p.m. or she will have to wait until midnight to enter.

Thank you very much.

J. Sekelow

UNIT
8

1. Why did Mr. Sekelow write to the gym?

    (A) To file a complaint

    (B) To apply for a position

    (C) To inquire about an event

    (D) To clarify the amount of the discount

2. Which is not true about J. Sekelow?

   (A) He intends to purchase two memberships.

   (B) He saw the advertisement in the end of December.

   (C) He may join the party with his girlfriend.

   (D) He can get a discount on his girlfriend's membership.

3. How much does Mr. Sekelow need to pay if he wants to buy two year fitness memberships for his girlfriend and himself?

   (A) $600

   (B) $680

   (C) $720

   (D) $800

4. In the advertisement, the word "complimentary" in paragraph 3, line 1, is closest in meaning to

   (A) limited

   (B) convenient

   (C) high-quality

   (D) free

5. Which membership can't Mr. Sekelow purchase?

   (A) One month

   (B) Twelve months

   (C) Two years

   (D) Three years

VI. Vocabulary Track-35–36

---

1. **manufacture** [ˌmænjuˋfæktʃɚ] v. 製造

Anthony is currently working in BBD, a company that **manufactures** car parts.

Anthony 目前任職於 BBD，一家製造汽車零件的公司。

---

2. **currently** [ˋkɝəntlɪ] adv. 現在；當今

Paisley is **currently** in Italy, negotiating a merger with another manufacturer.

Paisley 目前人在義大利，商議合併另一家製造商。

---

3. **party** [ˋpɑrtɪ] n. 當事人；一方

Though we have signed the contract with the manufacturing corporation, either **party** could terminate the contract any time.

雖然我們已經跟那間製造公司簽約，但任一方仍能隨時終止合約。

---

4. **extension** [ɪkˋstɛnʃən] n. 電話分機

To improve our company's internal communication, we add five more **extensions** in each office.　為了改善公司的內部溝通，我們在每個辦公室增設五個分機。

---

5. **expand** [ɪkˋspænd] v. 擴展；擴大

The board doesn't agree to **expand** the business in the current economic climate.

董事會不同意在目前的經濟情勢下擴張公司。

---

6. **state-of-the-art** [ˌstet əv ðə ˋɑrt] adj. 最先進的

This scanner uses **state-of-the-art** technology that makes scanning documents fast and easy.　這部掃描器應用了最先進的技術，讓掃描文件變得快速又簡單。

---

7. **supply** [səˋplaɪ] v. 供給

That newly built power plant **supplies** electricity to the two nearby cities.

那間最新完工的發電廠提供電力給鄰近的兩個城市。

UNIT
8

8. predict [prɪ`dɪkt] v. 預測；預料

Who could have **predicted** that the once small food company would become the leading one in food manufacturing?

誰能預料到曾經的一家小食品公司如今會成為食品製造業中的龍頭？

---

9. patent [`pætn̩t] n. 專利

Morgan finally obtained the **patent** on his invention.

Morgan 終於取得他的發明的專利。

---

10. utilize [`jutl̩͵aɪz] v. 利用；使用

The factory is trying to find more effective ways to **utilize** solar energy.

這間工廠正試圖尋找更有效的方法來使用太陽能。

---

11. application [͵æplə`keʃən] n. 應用；運用

This plastic material has many **applications**. You can find it in many different everyday objects.

這個塑膠原料有許多用途，你可以在許多不同的日常用品上看到它。

---

12. electricity [ɪ͵lɛk`trɪsətɪ] n. 電力

Almost all the machines in the car plant are powered by **electricity**.

汽車製造廠裡幾乎全部的機器都靠電力運轉。

---

13. majority [mə`dʒɔrətɪ] n. 大多數

The **majority** of the workers in this factory are proficient in maintaining their machinery.　工廠中多數工人都熟練於維護機器。

---

14. warehouse [`wɛr͵haʊs] n. 倉庫，貨倉

All the expensive leather goods are stored in this **warehouse**.

所有昂貴的皮革商品都被存放在這間倉庫裡。

15. **dimension** [də`mɛnʃən] n. 規模；維度

We are required to carefully measure the **dimensions** of our plant.

我們被要求仔細丈量我們工廠的大小。

16. **capability** [ˌkepə`bɪlətɪ] n. 功能；能力

The factory manager is demonstrating the technical **capabilities** of this newly developed machine. 工廠經理正在展示這部新開發機器所擁有的技術性能。

17. **complicated** [`kɑmpləˌketɪd] adj. 複雜的

One has to follow **complicated** instructions to run this machine.

要操作這部機器必須遵循複雜的指令。

18. **inspection** [ɪn`spɛkʃən] n. 檢查；檢驗

There will be an annual safety **inspection** on every elevator in our company tomorrow morning, so please take the stairs instead then.

明天早上將會執行公司電梯的年度安全檢查，屆時請使用樓梯上下樓。

19. **preferential** [ˌprɛfə`rɛnʃəl] adj. 優惠的；優先的

Consumers who place orders by the end of the month will receive **preferential** treatment—more discounts and an extended warranty.

在月底前下訂的消費者可享有優待—更多折扣及保固期延長。

20. **mutually** [`mjutʃuəlɪ] adv. 互相地；共同地

Continually growing in the existing market and entering a new market are not **mutually** exclusive strategies.

維持原有市場的成長與進入新市場並非相互排斥的策略。

UNIT
8

李海碩、張秀帆、多益 900 團隊 編著

Joseph E. Schier 審訂

專為學校課堂設計的多益學習教材

■涵蓋 2018 年 3 月最新改制多益題型。

■可全面提升所有學測考試題型之應試技巧。

■依難易度分為基礎篇與進階篇。

■隨書附贈解析本，內容包含完整中譯、題目解析及聽力腳本。

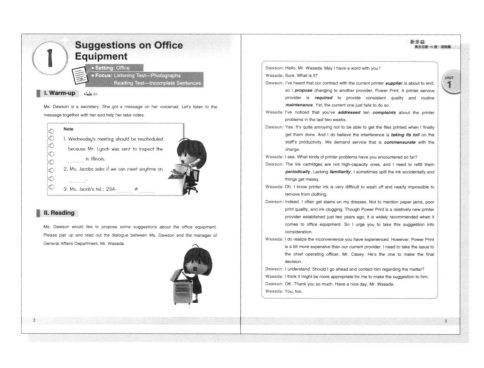

- 每單元介紹一個多益必考的生活或職場情境，並針對一項多益考題題型進行解題技巧教學。

- 學習活動取材自真實英語情境，完全模擬多益考題取材方向，並能讓你認識現實生活中英語的多樣面貌。

- 特別標記多益常考單字。幫助你快速掌握考試重點。

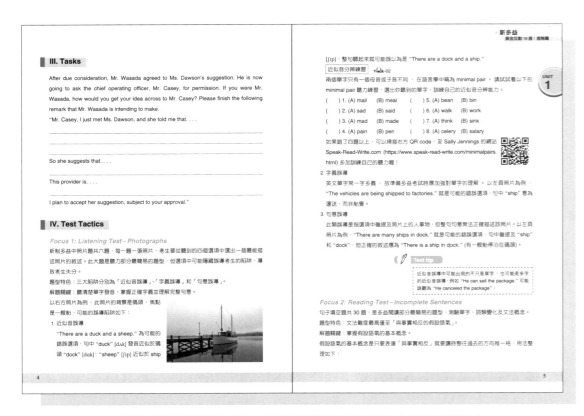

Intermediate Reading:

英文閱讀 High Five

掌握大考新趨勢，搶先練習新題型！

王隆興 編著

★全書分為 5 大主題：生態物種、人文歷史、科學科技、環境保育、醫學保健，共 50 篇由外籍作者精心編寫之文章。

★題目仿 111 學年度學測參考試卷命題方向設計，為未來大考提前作準備，搶先練習第二部分新題型——混合題。

★隨書附贈解析夾冊，方便練習後閱讀文章中譯及試題解析，並於解析補充每回文章精選的 15 個字彙。

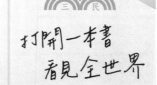

Let's TOEIC　可搭配108課綱加深加廣選修課程

NEW TOEIC

新多益

黃金互動16週：基礎篇 增訂二版
解析本

附電子朗讀音檔、解析本、模擬試題

李海碩、張秀帆、多益900團隊 編著
Joseph E. Schier 審定

三民書局

目次
Contents

Unit 1

I. Warm-up

Barbra Wayne

我需要一些建議。我明天要跟兩位重要客戶吃晚餐，現在正在找一家豪華、安靜、有品味的餐廳，當然要是一家有很棒的服務跟食物的。價錢不是問題。就像我剛剛說的，這兩位是非常重要的客戶。我的任務是讓他們有愉快的一晚。希望在佳餚、飲料以及一些極佳的甜點的幫助下，我能讓他們簽下合約。

Bobthesavior

如果你的客戶愛吃肉，我會建議去 Beefbelly。它從 1978 年就開始承辦宴席。在 Beefbelly 有各式各樣的牛排、三明治以及飲料。不過，他們的甜點不是特別出色。但你還是可以提供你的客戶們一頓美味的肉類大餐！

Miranda Wu

你一定要帶他們去 Chin Chin。Chin Chin 提供健康又美味的食物以及優質的服務。它供應各式各樣的菜餚來滿足所有消費者的口味。對吃素的人他們也有特製菜單。最重要的是，草莓塔和巧克力慕思是兩道必吃的甜點。

Pinkaya

我也會推薦 Chin Chin。他們的主廚總是按營養的食譜來烹調。他們不會用冷凍海鮮，所以他們海鮮的新鮮程度是*毋庸置疑*的。而且假如你的客戶會對任何食材過敏，只要事先跟店家說，他們就會照顧到你的需求。去之前記得先預約。他們常常客滿。

II. Reading

收件人：	Jenny McCoy <jennymccoy1802@kmail.com>
寄件人：	Barbra Wayne <bbwayne888@dmail.com>
日期：	11 月 14 日
主旨：	餐廳訂位

親愛的 Jenny：

我一直在思考餐廳的選擇，最後終於做出決定。可以請你幫我預約 Chin Chin 餐廳，明天晚上七點，六個人的位子嗎？我和我先生、我們老闆 Brian 和他太太以及兩位從法國來的客戶打算去用餐。

我是 Chin Chin 的常客。餐廳經理 Hank Reed 是我朋友。請告訴他，如果可能的話，我們想預約我們落地窗旁的老位子，這樣我們吃飯時就看得見游泳池。而且那個位子在一個寧靜的角落。我希望能在晚餐時談妥一份重要的交易，所以安靜的地方是必要的。

這兩位客人是我們公司重要的客戶，我想要把所有事情安排到完美。假如你沒辦法聯絡到 Reed 先生，就聯絡他的助理 Rebecca Myers。預約完成後請告知我一聲。

非常謝謝你。

Barbra

備註：其中一位客戶對螃蟹過敏。請記得告知餐廳經理這件事。

III. Tasks

A.

1. boss / supervisor

2. ☐ Call the restaurant and make a reservation for four.

☑ Call Hank Reed. If he isn't in, talk to Rebecca Myers instead.

☐ Make sure the table will be arranged as requested.

☐ Make sure the food order will be taken care of due to the client's allergy problem.

3. ☐ I'll see what I can do.

☐ I'm pleased to inform you that the product you ordered has arrived.

☐ No problem. Our restaurant is booked up.

☐ I'll inform the kitchen to avoid crab dishes that evening.

☐ I'm afraid we're fully booked that evening.

☐ Of course we can reserve that table for you.

B. E

IV. Test Tactics

第一類

練習 1

名詞：woman, drink, beverage, liquid, cup, kitchen, pitcher

動詞：prepare, pour, work, hold

練習 2

The woman is preparing drinks / beverages.

The woman is pouring some liquid into a cup.

The woman is working in the kitchen.

The woman is holding two cups / a pitcher and a cup.

第二類

練習 1

名詞：fork, napkin, plate, glass, plant

形容詞：clean, neat, empty

介係詞：on, to, in front of

練習 2

The forks are placed on the clean napkins.

To the right of each plate are a fork, a napkin, and a glass.

An empty glass is placed in front of the plant.

- -

練習 1

名詞：people, restaurant, dish, waiter, wine, curtains

動詞：dine, serve, look at, smile

介係詞：in, in front of, on

練習 2

People are dining in the restaurant.

The dishes have been served.

The waiter is serving wine.

The man is looking at the dishes in front of him and smiling.

There are curtains on the wall.

(答案僅供參考)

V. Learn by Doing

| 1. A | 2. A | 3. D | 4. C | 5. B | 6. B | 7. C | 8. D |

聽力腳本

1. (A) The table has been set.
   (B) The dishes are all empty.
   (C) The guests are sitting at the table.
   (D) The banquet is coming to the end.
   (A) 桌面已擺設好。
   (B) 碗盤都空了。
   (C) 客人們都坐在桌旁。
   (D) 筵席即將結束。

2. (A) The catering service is operating.
   (B) The **refreshments** haven't arrived.
   (C) The waiter is wearing a hat.
   (D) The guests are seated to be served.
   (A) 正在提供餐飲服務。
   (B) 點心還沒到。
   (C) 服務生戴著一頂帽子。
   (D) 客人們都已就座，等待服務。

3. (A) The woman is buying poultry.
   (B) The woman is at the dairy section.
   (C) The woman is preparing some beverages.
   (D) The woman is shopping for fruits.
   (A) 女子正在買雞肉。
   (B) 女子在乳製品區。
   (C) 女子正在準備飲料。
   (D) 女子正在買水果。

4. (A) The couple is at the **reception** desk.
   (B) The waitress is serving the main course.
   (C) The waiter is serving the wine for the couple.
   (D) The couple is enjoying their main course.
   (A) 這對情侶在櫃臺前。

   (B) 女服務生正在上主菜。
   (C) 服務生正在幫這對情侶上酒。
   (D) 這對情侶正在享用主菜。

5. (A) The chef is having the cuisine.
   (B) The chef is preparing the cuisine.
   (C) The chef is looking for the right ingredient.
   (D) The chef has frozen the dish.
   (A) 主廚正在用餐。
   (B) 主廚正在準備料理。
   (C) 主廚正在尋找正確的食材。
   (D) 主廚把這道菜肴冷凍好了。

6. (A) The woman is talking on the phone.
   (B) The woman is reading a recipe.
   (C) The woman is cutting the vegetable.
   (D) The woman is cutting the pizza.
   (A) 女子正在講電話。
   (B) 女子正在讀食譜。
   (C) 女子正在切菜。
   (D) 女子正在切披薩。

7. (A) The **cafeteria** is empty.
   (B) The students are taking a test.
   (C) The students are getting food in line.
   (D) The students are taking a **culinary** class.
   (A) 自助餐廳裡沒有人。
   (B) 學生們正在考試。
   (C) 學生們正在排隊拿食物。
   (D) 學生在正在上烹飪課。

8. (A) The woman is writing a recipe.
   (B) The woman is taking out some frozen food.

(C) The woman is making reservations.

(D) The woman is reading labels on the package.

(A) 女子正在寫食譜。

(B) 女子正把冷凍食品拿出來。

(C) 女子正在進行預訂。

(D) 女子正在讀商品上的標籤。

Unit 2

I. Warm-up

The interviewee is Bob Rose.

聽力腳本

W: Can you tell me why you are applying for the assistant manager in our company?

M: Well, the company I'm currently working for is quite small. It's an eight-person company. I'd like to work somewhere larger with more opportunities to deal with cases and to cooperate with people. And of course, an opportunity to travel, if possible. I'd like the challenge to push myself further.

W: Do you think a larger company will be a better match for you?

M: Yes, I believe so. I think it will give me some valuable and unique work experience.

W: In our company, we often work in teams. How do you feel about that?

M: I prefer working with others to working by myself, so it would be great to be part of a team.

W: OK. That'll be all for this interview. I'll give you our decision by this Friday.

M: Thank you. I'm looking forward to hearing from you.

女：請問為什麼你想應徵我們公司的副理職位呢？

男：嗯，我目前工作的公司很小。是一間八人公司。我想要在一間更大間、有更多機會處理案子以及與人合作的公司工作。當然，可能的話也希望有出差的機會。我想要多挑戰自己、精進自己。

女：你覺得較大型的公司會更適合你嗎？

男：對，我確信是這樣。我認為大公司會帶給我一些有價值又獨特的工作經驗。

女：我們公司通常是以團隊的方式工作。你對這樣的工作模式有什麼看法？

男：比起單打獨鬥，我更喜歡跟其他人並肩作戰，所以能成為團隊的一分子是很棒的。

女：好的。面試大致到這裡結束。我會在這星期五前通知你我們的決定。

男：謝謝。我很期待收到您的消息。

II. Reading

Bennet 小姐：早安，Lynch 先生。請坐。

Lynch 先生：謝謝。叫我 James 就好。

Bennet 小姐：好的。我是人事主管 Helen Bennet。我看了你的履歷，你想應徵的是副理職位對吧？

Lynch 先生：是的，沒錯。

Bennet 小姐：可以談談你的工作經驗嗎？

Lynch 先生：好的。我現在在一家中型食品公司 Joyce 擔任專案經理。

Bennet 小姐：喔，我知道 Joyce 食品公司。是一家小而優質的公司。

Lynch 先生：沒錯。在 Joyce 食品公司工作前，我在一家電子公司的業務部門擔任組長。我有十二年的工作經驗，接觸過許多不同類型的產業。

Bennet 小姐：那真不錯。請問為什麼你對我們 Green 食品公司有興趣呢？

Lynch 先生：嗯，我只是覺得我應該有些進步。我已經在我目前的工作做了四年，現在該是我繼續前進、追尋新挑戰的時候了。因為你們公司注重客戶服務，這是我的專長之一，我想我非常適合你們公司。

Bennet 小姐：好的。在這個職位會有很多時候要跟其他人進行團隊合作。你能和別人建立良好的合作關係嗎？

Lynch 先生：是的！我喜歡團隊合作。

Bennet 小姐：很好。最後，可以給我要僱用你的理由嗎？

Lynch 先生：我擅長發想新的專案，而且我不介意在必要時加班。

Bennet 小姐：嗯，謝謝你今天來面試。在面試其他的應試者後，我們一旦有了決定就會通知你。

Lynch 先生：謝謝您今天讓我來面試。非常期待接到您的消息。

III. Tasks

A. Assistant manager; James; Lynch; Project manager; 12; 3300 USD (答案僅供參考)

IV. Test Tactics

> 1. A　2. C　3. D　4. C　5. A　6. B　7. C　8. C　9. B

聽力腳本

Questions 1 through 3 refer to the following conversation.

W: Hey, Jack. Are you still able to join our daily study group this afternoon? It would be good to have you there.

M: Sure, I can make it. I'll definitely be there on time. Are we still meeting in the study room on the second floor of the library today?

W: No, we aren't. That room has been booked by another group of students. We've changed our meeting location to the third floor of the library, room 309.

M: Thanks for letting me know. Oh, by the way, I've done some research on business *ethics*. I'll share my findings with you this afternoon.

請參考以下的對話回答第 1 題至 3 題。

女：嘿，Jack。你今天下午還能參加我們的每日讀書會嗎？如果你能來的話就太棒了。

男：好啊，我可以參加。我一定會準時出席。我們今天一樣在圖書館二樓的閱覽室舉行讀書會嗎？

女：不是。閱覽室今天被另一群學生先預約了。我們已經把讀書會地點改到圖書館三樓的 309 室。

男：謝謝你讓我知道。喔，順帶一提，我已經針對商業倫理做了一些研究。今天下午我會和你們分享我的研究發現。

Questions 4 through 6 refer to the following conversation.

M: Good morning. I am calling to inquire about the vacancy in the sales department.

W: Sure, there are two positions that need to be filled in international sales. Do you speak any foreign languages?

M: I speak French rather well and can speak some Spanish.

W: We have needs with both languages. Could you please forward me your résumé? If invited for an interview, you will need to display your *proficiency* in at least French.

請參考以下的對話回答第 4 題至 6 題。

男：早安。我打電話是想詢問一下業務部的職缺。

女：好的，現在國際業務有兩個職缺在徵人。你會說任何外語嗎？

男：我法語說的不錯，也會說一點西班牙語。

女：這兩種語言我們都需要。可以寄給我你的履歷嗎？假如進到面試程序，你會需要至少展現你的法語程度。

Questions 7 through 9 refer to the following conversation.

M: Excuse me, madam. My computer has been playing up, and sometimes shuts down automatically while I'm using it. I'm eager to get a new one.

W: It's a pleasure to be of service to you. Have you taken a look at the new Melon computers that have come out recently? They're 10% off.

M: I noticed that, but I read on one of your brochures that you are selling some Tokuba computers that are 20% off.

W: Yes, we have several computers with a 20% discount. However, they aren't the latest models. Laptops like these ones, on the other hand, come with features such as touch screens and voice commands. Here, let me demonstrate how to use them.

請參考以下的對話回答第 7 題至 9 題。

男：不好意思，女士。我的電腦故障了，有時候用到一半就自動關機。我想買一臺新的。

女：為您服務是我的榮幸。您有參考過 Melon 電腦最近才推出的新機型嗎？現在打九折。

男：我有注意到，但我看到你們的廣告冊上寫說你們這裡 Tokuba 電腦現在打八折。

女：對，我們有幾臺電腦在打八折。不過，它們並不是最新款的。像這邊的新型筆記型電腦就有觸控式螢幕跟聲控功能。來讓我來展示一下怎麼使用這些功能吧！

V. Learn by Doing

| 1. A | 2. C | 3. D | 4. B | 5. C | 6. D | 7. D | 8. B | 9. A | 10. C | 11. A | 12. A | 13. C | 14. A | 15. D |

聽力腳本

Questions 1 through 3 refer to the following conversation.

M: Are you positive that we are going in the right direction to our hotel? It seems to be taking a lot longer than we expected, and I'm concerned we won't arrive on time.

W: I was sure this is the right direction, but now I'm confused. I was given clear directions on a map that can guide me straight to the hotel, but it's a pity I forgot to bring them.

M: I think it would be best if we stop and ask someone for clearer directions. There is an information center on the left. It is possible that someone there can guide us in the right direction.

請參考以下的對話回答第 1 題至 3 題。

男：你確定我們現在去飯店的路是正確的嗎？好像比我們預想的路還要長，我擔心我們無法準時到達。

女：我本來很確定這是對的路，但現在我有點搞混了。地圖上給的指示可以帶我們直接到達飯店，但很遺憾，我忘記帶了。

男：我想最好的辦法是我們停下來找人詢問較明確的方向。左手邊有一個服務中心。那邊可能會有人能夠指引我們正確的方向。

1. 男子在擔心什麼？

   (A) 無法準時到飯店   (B) 無法找到停車位   (C) 沒有看懂地圖   (D) 必須付額外的錢

2. 女子忘記帶什麼？

   (A) 飯店的照片   (B) 飯店的地址   (C) 去飯店的路線   (D) 住飯店的錢

3. 為什麼男子想停下來？

   (A) 買新地圖   (B) 打電話給飯店   (C) 吃一下晚餐   (D) 尋求幫助

Questions 4 through 6 refer to the following conversation.

W1: Hello, could I speak with Mr. Xiao? It's regarding the construction of the Central Bank in Brisbane City. He's the head manager of this project, right?

W2: Yes, but could you please tell me who's calling?

W1: Ms. Andrews speaking. I'm the purchasing manager of Farthest Construction Company.

W2: OK, I'll transfer you to Mr. Xiao. Please wait a moment, madam.

W1: Thanks.

M: Hello? Ms. Andrews?

W1: Hello, Mr. Xiao. I'm ordering the wood for the ceiling this morning, but I don't have the blueprint for the first and second floor.

M: OK, I'll print the blueprint for you. Would you be able to come into my office tomorrow morning by 11 o'clock? It will be ready by then.

請參考以下的對話回答第 4 題至 6 題。

女 1：喂，請問蕭先生在嗎？我要跟他談關於布里斯本中央銀行建設案的事。他是這個專案的總負責人對吧？

女 2：是的，請問您哪裡找？

女 1：我是 Andrews 小姐。我是 Farthest 建設公司的採購經理。

女 2：好的，我幫您轉接給蕭先生。請您稍等一下。

女 1：謝謝。

男：喂？Andrews 小姐嗎？

女 1：喂，蕭先生。我今天早上要訂購天花板的木材，但我沒有一樓跟二樓的設計藍圖。

男：好的。我會印藍圖給你。你明天早上十一點前可以來我的辦公室嗎？那個時候應該會弄好。

4. 蕭先生是誰？

   (A) 建築工人   (B) 專案經理   (C) 祕書   (D) 採購經理

5. Andrews 小姐遇到什麼問題？

   (A) 她想不到要如何設計那家銀行。   (B) 有一項測量數據不正確。

   (C) 她沒有設計藍圖。   (D) 她訂錯了建材。

6. Andrews 小姐需要做什麼？

   (A) 重畫藍圖   (B) 繼續找設計圖

   (C) 重新設計一樓和二樓   (D) 明天拜訪蕭先生的辦公室

Questions 7 through 9 refer to the following conversation.

W: We've chosen a suitable marketing company to advertise our newly manufactured cars. The COO of this company will be making us a visit in two weeks from now, and I am making plans for them to attend a detailed tour of our production line on Wednesday morning. I hope that's okay.

M: Let me see. Well, we are planning on doing an inspection of our production machinery on Wednesday. I would suggest that we make it next Thursday.

W: Sure. The company's COO will leave around Thursday afternoon, so I think we will be able to fit in a basic tour during the morning. I'll contact the COO now to confirm if this time change is alright with him.

請參考以下的對話回答第 7 題至 9 題。

女：我們已經選了適合的行銷公司來推廣我們最新出廠的車。這家公司的營運長在接下來的兩週內會來拜訪我們，所以我正規畫星期三早上讓他們完整參觀我們的生產線。希望這樣沒問題。

男：我看一下。嗯，我們預計在星期三檢查生產線的機器。我建議把參訪的時間改成下星期四。

女：好的。對方公司的營運長大概星期四下午會離開，所以我想我們能剛好在當天早上安排一趟簡單的參訪。我現在就聯絡營運長，看這樣的時間調整他是否可接受。

7. 誰預計要來拜訪這家製造商？
   (A) 粉刷公司的營運長
   (B) 法律事務所的執行長
   (C) 製造公司的執行長
   (D) 行銷公司的營運長

8. 為什麼男子建議另一天？
   (A) 他們計畫要粉刷工廠。
   (B) 他們將檢查生產機器。
   (C) 他們將進行生產線導覽。
   (D) 他們將召開機密會議。

9. 女子接下來可能要做什麼？
   (A) 詢問營運長下星期四是否可以來
   (B) 取消營運長的拜訪
   (C) 打電話給行銷公司的執行長
   (D) 拜訪行銷公司

Questions 10 through 12 refer to the following conversation.

M: Would you be able to spare several minutes to discuss the results of the sales training presentation I gave last week?

W1: Of course! I received a lot of good feedback. Many people said your presentation was helpful for them in the workplace and packed with practical tips for doing sales.

W2: But some also mentioned that several points in your presentation were not clearly explained. I suggest you slow down when you emphasize a key point and find examples that are easy to grasp.

M: Good idea! I'll take your advice into **consideration** next time I give a presentation. In the future, I'll also make some slight adjustments to the gestures I use when emphasizing key points.

請參考以下的對話回答第 10 題至 12 題。

男：你們可以騰出幾分鐘來討論一下我上週業務訓練演說的結果嗎？

女 1：當然！我收到好多正面評價。很多人都說你的演說對他們在職場上很有幫助，而且演說裡含有好多做業務的實用祕訣。

女 2：不過有些人也提到你演說中有幾個論點並沒有清楚解釋。建議你在強調重點的時候要放慢語速，並且舉一些容易理解的例子。

男：好主意！下次演講的時候，我會把你的建議納入考慮。未來我也會在強調重點時稍微調整一下我的手勢。

10. 男子的演說是關於哪一方面的？
    (A) 電子設備　　　　(B) 人力資源　　　　(C) 業務　　　　(D) 管理

11. 聽眾們給了什麼正面的回饋？

(A) 演說很有幫助。　　　　　　　　　　(B) 舉的例子很有力。

(C) 演說架構完整。　　　　　　　　　　(D) 男子很有自信。

12. 男子想做什麼改進？

(A) 調整他的手勢　　　(B) 提供更多重點　　　(C) 講得更快　　　(D) 使用較少手勢

Questions 13 through 15 refer to the following conversation.

M: Hi Andrea, this is Mr. Johnson, the editor of *Explorer* magazine. Can we talk now?

W: Sure.

M: I was wondering if you could change the length of the article "Discovering Desert Islands" to 2,500 words.

W: That shouldn't be a big problem, as I have more to write on that topic. The problem is that the due date for another article falls on the same day.

M: OK. Let's postpone the deadline for that article by two weeks. That way, you'll have time to work on "Discovering Desert Islands".

W: Thanks a million. By the way, I've been coming up with some ideas for the article on Hawaii. I'll email them to you tomorrow.

請參考以下的對話回答第 13 題至 15 題。

男：嗨，Andrea，我是 Johnson 先生，《探險者》雜誌的編輯。現在方便說話嗎？

女：可以。

男：我在想你是否可以把「發現荒島」這篇文章的長度改成兩千五百字？

女：那應該不是大問題，因為對這個主題我也有更多東西可以寫。問題是有另一篇文章的截稿日也在同一天。

男：好。那我們把那篇文章的截止日期延後兩星期吧。這樣一來，你就有時間來處理「發現荒島」了。

女：萬分感謝。順帶一提，我有一些關於夏威夷那篇文章的想法。明天會寄到你的電子信箱。

文章標題	截止期限
長毛象的突變	一月十一日
夏威夷傳奇	四月十二日
發現荒島	三月十日
看不見的世界	三月十日

13. 哪篇文章需要被加長？

(A)「長毛象的突變」　　(B)「夏威夷傳奇」　　(C)「發現荒島」　　(D)「看不見的世界」

14. 請參照圖表。哪篇文章的截止日期會被調整？

(A)「看不見的世界」　　(B)「發現荒島」　　(C)「夏威夷傳奇」　　(D)「長毛象的突變」

15. 女子將會寄給男子什麼？

(A) 關於長毛象突變的新文章　　　　　　(B) 荒島的照片

(C)「看不見的世界」的相關資訊　　　　(D) 有關夏威夷文章的想法

Unit 3

I. Warm-up

編號	商品描述	數量	每單位價格 (美元)	總額 (美元)
	Robin & Robert Medical 公司 **文具訂購單**			
1	筆–藍	500		
2	鉛筆–2B	250		
3	釘書機	100		
4	標籤	40 包		
5	紙–A4	200 包		

II. Reading

給全體員工的通知

好消息！Venus Press 今年業績已有百分之二十的成長，而且還達成了令人難以置信的目標：我們的年度業績超過兩千萬元！為了獎勵各位的努力和投入，每個月都會有辦公室文具的採購。

新的安排如下：
- 每個部門的助理會在每月五號前透過採購部門下訂單。
- 每個部門一個月最多可以下十筆訂單或者達到五百美元的訂單總額。
- 每位員工皆要填寫採購單來告知助理自己的需求。
- 一年中訂購最少的部門將會得到 Mary 百貨公司的的禮券。

以上的安排是暫時性的。在試行三個月後，我們會審視這項政策並評估是否需要做任何改變。

採購部

III. Tasks

Yes, the policy is fantastic! We no longer need to worry about the shortage of supplies. With plenty of stationery, we can focus more on our work, and we'll be able to work more efficiently.

However, I'm afraid there might be a problem if people waste the office supplies or start taking them home. (答案僅供參考)

IV. Test Tactics

Step 1.

> 1. A   2. C   3. A

聽力腳本

1. Whose smartphone is this?

    (A) It belongs to our manager.

    (B) It's out of stock.

(C) It's advanced technology.

這是誰的智慧型手機？

(A) 是我們經理的。

(B) 它缺貨。

(C) 是先進的科技。

2. You brought that voucher, didn't you?

(A) I'll vote tomorrow.

(B) It's a great deal

(C) I surely did.

你帶了禮券來，沒帶嗎？

(A) 我明天會去投票。

(B) 這很划算。

(C) 我確定帶了。

3. I'd like to get a **refund**.

(A) Sure. Please give me the receipt.

(B) You need to pay in cash.

(C) 20% discount.

我想退錢。

(A) 好的，請給我收據。

(B) 您必須以現金付款。

(C) 八折。

Step 2.

2. B
Possible responses: I like it so much. It was quite interesting / entertaining. It wasn't to my taste. It was boring. It was too long to sustain my interest. 3. A Possible responses: Sure, that's a good idea. I'd like to, but I'll be tied up. Sorry, I've got something else to do. No, I have to work overtime tomorrow. I'm afraid we can't. (答案僅供參考)

聽力腳本

1. Did you get lots of bargains at the clearance sale?

(A) He didn't want to bargain with me.

(B) Yes, everything was half-price.

(C) They are clearing up the store.

你在清倉大拍賣買到很多便宜貨嗎？

(A) 他不想跟我討價還價。

(B) 對，每件商品都半價。

(C) 他們在清掃店面。

2. How did you enjoy the movie last night?

(A) I watched it around 8 p.m.

(B) It was quite thrilling.

(C) I had to work overtime.

你覺得昨天晚上的電影如何？

(A) 我大概晚上八點去看的。

(B) 電影相當刺激。

(C) 我得加班。

3. Can we go to that anniversary sale tomorrow?

(A) No, I'm flat out busy tomorrow.

(B) It's our second anniversary.

(C) Everything is on sale.

我們明天可以去週年慶大拍賣嗎？

(A) 不行，我明天實在太忙了。

(B) 那是我們的兩週年紀念日。

(C) 每件商品都在打折。

Step 3.

Response	Possible Question
b. It takes 20 minutes to walk there.	How long does it take to go to the department store?
c. It's across from the post office.	Where is the stationery store? Do you know where the supermarket is? Could you tell me where the hospital is?
d. I live in this district.	Where do you live?
e. With his wife.	Who did John come to the party with? Who does John live with? Who is John arguing with?
f. You may ask the store manager.	Whom should I ask about the price? Do you have vacancies for stockroom assistants? May I inquire how much it is?
g. It's too high to me.	What would you say about the price? What's your opinion of the cost? What do you think about the risk?
h. Yes, of course.	Could you show me how to use this appliance? Could you help me with the box? Can I reserve a table for five for 12:00?
i. I would love to.	Would you like to join the party? Would you like to come to dinner with us? Would you like to have some coffee? (答案僅供參考)

1. A 2. C 3. A

聽力腳本

1. When will John come to the party?

(A) In another 30 minutes.

(B) I would love to.

(C) With his wife.

John 會什麼時候來派對？

(A) 再三十分鐘後。

(B) 我想要。

(C) 跟他太太一起。

2. Who should I consult about the price of this appliance?

(A) It's too high to me.

(B) Yes, of course.

(C) You may ask the store manager.

我應該跟誰諮詢這臺家電的價格？

(A) 對我來說太貴了。

(B) 對，當然。

(C) 你可以去問店長。

3. Where's the convenience store located in this district?

   (A) It's across from the post office.

   (B) I live in this district.

   (C) It takes 20 minutes to walk there.

這區的便利商店在哪裡呢？

(A) 在郵局對面。

(B) 我住在這一區。

(C) 走路大概要花二十分鐘。

V. Learn by Doing

1. B 2. B 3. C 4. A 5. B 6. A 7. B 8. C 9. B 10. A

聽力腳本

1. How long is the *warranty* for this washing machine?

   (A) About two weeks ago.

   (B) Twenty-four months.

   (C) It comes free of charge.

這臺洗衣機的保固期有多久？

(A) 大概兩星期前。

(B) 二十四個月。

(C) 這是免費取得的。

2. Is your manager coming in today or next week?

   (A) He enjoyed his business trip.

   (B) He's in the office next week.

   (C) That's not quite right.

你們經理今天或下週會在嗎？

(A) 他出差很愉快。

(B) 他下週會在辦公室。

(C) 那不太對勁。

3. When will I be able to obtain my license, next month or in two months?

   (A) I got it last year.

   (B) I already have a driver's license.

   (C) Within three months.

我什麼時候能拿到我的執照？下個月還是兩個月內？

(A) 我去年就拿到了。

(B) 我已經有駕照了。

(C) 三個月內。

4. Do you offer an operation *manual* for this item?

   (A) It's in the package.

   (B) The description isn't clear enough.

   (C) It's difficult to operate.

你們提供這項產品的操作手冊嗎？

(A) 它在包裝裡。

(B) 敘述不夠清楚。

(C) 它很不好操作。

5. What do you think about online *consumer behavior?*

   (A) That would be nice.

   (B) Quite complicated.

   (C) You should behave well.

你對線上的消費者行為有什麼想法嗎？

(A) 那會是很不錯的。

(B) 那相當複雜。

(C) 你應該好好表現。

6. Are there any washing machines in stock here?

   (A) Sorry, they are sold out already.

   (B) The stock prices have fallen.

   (C) We have a laundry service.

這裡還有任何洗衣機的庫存嗎？

(A) 很抱歉，洗衣機都已經賣完了。

(B) 股價已經下跌了。

(C) 我們有洗衣服務。

7. How long did you linger in front of that store?

   (A) It still lingers in my memory.

   (B) Just for one or two minutes.

   (C) The cat was in front of the store.

你在那家店前面徘徊了多久？

(A) 它還在我記憶中縈繞。

(B) 只有一兩分鐘而已。

(C) 貓在店前面。

8. Will you introduce me to the wholesale supplier?

(A) We sell goods to local stores.

(B) We don't supply those goods.

(C) Maybe another time.

你能把我介紹給批發供應商嗎？

(A) 我們賣東西給當地的商家。

(B) 我們不提供那些商品。

(C) 也許下次吧。

9. Would you mind if we order thirty kilograms of wheat in bulk?

(A) Yes, I'll send you the book.

(B) Sure, when would you like them delivered?

(C) I'd like a receipt.

我們可以下三十公斤小麥的訂單嗎？

(A) 對，我會把書寄給您。

(B) 當然可以，您希望它們什麼時候送到？

(C) 我想要收據。

10. Don't you know how to operate the printer?

(A) I was hoping you could show me.

(B) No, he can't use it.

(C) It's my pleasure.

你不知道怎麼操作這臺印表機嗎？

(A) 我剛剛正希望你可以操作給我看。

(B) 不會，他不會用。

(C) 這是我的榮幸。

Unit 4

I. Warm-up

A. PC (personal computer)

B. HDD (hard disc drive)

C. external hard drive

D. CDs

E. printer

F. ink cartridges

G. fax machine

H. laptop

I. USB

J. speakers

The former secretary gave Adam ___C___.

所有的檔案，尤其是那些機密檔案，都必須要同時在電腦桌面上儲存並在外接硬碟備份。外接硬碟的容量很大，有 3TB。你可以用 2.0 或 3.0 的 USB 接頭把它連結到你的電腦。雖然這個外接硬碟能夠儲存各種檔案，但是請只要儲存與工作相關的檔案。

請好好存放這個硬碟，避免硬碟受損以及資料流失。此外，使用前請仔細閱讀下面的指示！

✓ 當硬碟還在運作或仍連接在電腦上的時候，請勿移動硬碟。

✓ 當硬碟運作了一段長時間，例如一個小時，硬碟可能會變得很熱。別擔心。這是完全正常的，而且它的先進設計會讓它很快冷卻下來。

✓ 請勿嘗試打開硬碟的外殼。

✓ 請勿在硬碟上堆放任何東西或把硬碟側放。這些動作都可能會使它受損。

✓ 定期檢測硬碟並刪除不需要的檔案。

祝你新工作順利！

II. Reading

收件人：	Brian's Brain 公司員工
寄件人：	Ruth Henderson
日期：	12 月 23 日
主旨：	請款單
附件：	請款單表格

親愛的同仁：

在此緊急通知你，必須在年底前提交你的請款單。請確認在提交請款單時要一併附上所有消費的單據。除了娛樂支出，旅行支出、住宿費及伙食費可以直接列在請款單上。填寫請款單時，請務必記得填上你的員工編號以加速請款流程。你將會在下個月月底前收到請款的款項。

請見附件的請款單表格。填好表格後，請在十二月三十一日前把表格和收據放在我的桌上，或把它們交給任一位出納組的員工。最後但同樣重要的是，別忘了自己留存一份請款單副本。

謝謝，並祝新年快樂！

出納組主管
Ruth Henderson

III. Tasks

Brian's Brain Co. Employees' Expense Report

Purpose: _Software testing for banks_   Statement Number: 45015864582

Employee Information:

Name: Abraham Lucas   Employee ID Number: TS890443227

Department: Technology   Position: Software Engineer

Date	Description	Hotel	Transport	Meals
11/13–14	Hotel (1 night)	$317.40		
11/13	Dinner			$85.80
			TOTAL	$403.20

V. Learn by Doing

1. A 2. C 3. A 4. D 5. C

請參考以下的調查回答第 1 題至 2 題。

Tutor DEF 教師培訓系列研習會
研習會：四種教授兒童英語的方法
參加者姓名：John Bradson

請選出至少兩個您選擇參加這次研習會的理由。
　　☐ 我的教學技巧還不到水準。
　　☑ 我想要瞭解更多關於兒童教育的事情。
　　☑ 我想在這個領域賺到更多錢。
　　☑ 我想知道兒童補習班如何運作。
　　☐ 我想在英語教學方面超越自己。
　　☐ 我只是想完成這個科目的一門課程。

請表達您是否同意以下的敘述。

	同意	不同意
演講者的說明很容易理解。	☐	☑
演講者安排的研習會內容符合您的需求。	☑	☐
我得到的知識和技巧非常有用且實際。	☑	☐

供改進參考的建議：
雖然知識非常實用，但演講者也許需要修正他傳遞課程內容的方式，並且讓整體內容簡短一些。

1. 關於講座的內容，文中提及了什麼？
　　(A) 關於如何教兒童英語。
　　(B) 關於如何創立一家補習班。
　　(C) 以企業領導為主題。
　　(D) 關於行政管理。

2. Bradson 先生對這位演講者提出了什麼建議？
　　(A) 他應該增進自己關於這個主題的認識。
　　(B) 他應該把知識變得更加實用。
　　(C) 他應該更簡短扼要地呈現他的資料。
　　(D) 他投影片的組織架構應該要做得更好。

請參考以下的電子郵件回答第 3 題至 5 題。

收件人：	Anthony Rogerson
寄件人：	Engeo 公司副理 George Frankson
主旨：	你所購買的機器的操作
日期：	九月二十七日

親愛的 Rogerson 先生：

我來信是想和您說明關於上週您向我們公司採購的機器。首先，我們為每臺機器都提供了操作手冊。遵循指示並定期檢查機器是否受損是非常重要的。您可以複印機器的操作手冊並將手冊分發給您部門的所有工作人員。如果機器因為錯誤的使用而受損，我們將不會給予賠償。如果機器故障，請馬上通知我們。我們可以提供協助來修復機器。不要嘗試自己修理機器，因為情況可能只會變得更糟。

若您的工作人員在閱讀操作手冊之後還是不確定如何操作機器的話，我們可以安排一位專業人員去為你們做一次基礎示範。如果您對於我們的售後服務有任何問題，歡迎留言給我。我將會儘快回覆您。

3. 這封電子郵件的目的是什麼？
   (A) 提供客戶售後服務　　　　　　　　(B) 推廣機器
   (C) 宣布機器模型的改變　　　　　　　(D) 送出一些機器的訂單

4. 如果機器故障，Rogerson 先生應該做什麼？
   (A) 打電話給另一家修理公司　　　　　(B) 嘗試自己修理機器
   (C) 研讀操作手冊　　　　　　　　　　(D) 立即聯絡 Frankson 先生

5. 關於這臺機器的敘述，何者正確？
   (A) 操作手冊上沒提到如何操作這臺機器。　(B) 這臺機器如果受損是無法修理的。
   (C) 這臺機器必須小心操作。　　　　　　　(D) 這臺機器使用起來很危險。

Unit 5

I. Warm-up

☐ How long the performance is
☑ The title of the performance
☑ How long the break during the play is
☐ The time the performance ends
☐ How many people are attending the show
☐ The time the performance begins
☑ What people can do during the intermission
☑ What people can buy in the theater
☑ What people can't do during the performance

先生女士們，晚安。歡迎來到 Royal 電影院。今天晚上，我們非常榮幸能為各位呈現最受好評的經典音樂劇《貓》。希望您會喜歡。請注意，不論照相或錄影都是被嚴格禁止的。表演期間，請將您的手機關機。表演分為上半場和下半場，中場休息為二十分鐘。中場休息時，在大廳會準備輕食供您選購。提醒您，觀眾席上禁止飲食。謝謝。祝您有個美好的一晚。

II. Reading

DMS 電影院——《星際幻想》電影系列馬拉松暨影展 八月十六日至二十一日
這星期來 DMS 電影院重溫經典電影吧！《星際幻想》電影系列的影迷們，來參加這場盛事，你會受到震撼！

	首部曲《帝國崛起》	二部曲《革命的代價》	三部曲《亞比該公主》
一廳	09:30　12:30　15:30 19:30　21:30　23:30	10:00　13:00　16:00 19:00　22:00　24:00	09:00　12:00　15:00 17:30　19:30　22:30
	四部曲《複製人之流》	五部曲《少年的覺醒》	六部曲《和平》
二廳	09:30　12:30　15:30 19:30　21:30　23:30	10:00　13:00　16:00 19:00　22:00　24:00	09:00　12:00　15:00 17:30　19:30　22:30

	首部曲 《帝國崛起》			二部曲 《革命的代價》			三部曲 《亞比該公主》		
三廳	10:00	13:00	16:00	09:00	12:00	15:00	09:30	12:30	15:30
	19:00	22:00	24:00	17:30	19:30	22:30	19:30	21:30	23:30
	四部曲 《複製人之流》			五部曲 《少年的覺醒》			六部曲 《和平》		
四廳	10:00	13:00	16:00	09:00	12:00	15:00	09:30	12:30	15:30
	19:00	22:00	24:00	17:30	19:30	22:30	19:30	21:30	23:30

※ 特展—Crystal 展廳 (六樓)

　　展出電影周邊商品、服裝、雕像和海報收藏。歡迎至第一展覽室購買吸引人的限量版商品。

※ 特別見面會

　　最新一級電影《和平》的製作人及導演將於八月十八日與熱情的粉絲們見面！購買套票的粉絲們將可免費入場！

III. Tasks

A. ☐ see episodes I to VI　　　　　　　☑ buy package tickets

　　☐ buy merchandise of the movies　　☐ wait in line on the night of August 17

B.

Thu. 8/16	✓ *18:00–20:00 dinner with Jenny* ✓ *21:30 Theater 1, Episode I*	**Sun. 8/19**	✓ *18:00–21:00 men's night* ✓ 13:00 Theater 2, Episode V
Fri. 8/17	✓ *17:00–21:00 work overtime* ✓ *21:30 pub date* ✓ 24:00 Theater 1, Episode II	**Mon. 8/20**	✓ *22:00–23:00 play basketball*
Sat. 8/18	✓ 15:00 Theater 1, Episode III ✓ 19:30 Theater 2, Episode IV	**Tue. 8/21**	✓ 19:30 Theater 4, Episode VI (僅供參考，此活動無標準答案)

V. Learn by Doing

1. C　2. A　3. A　4. B　5. A　6. D　7. B　8. B　9. A

1. 汽車零件展已被延後至下星期三。

　　(A) 是 (過去式)　　　　　(B) 將　　　　　　　(C) 已經　　　　　　(D) 是 (現在式)

2. 雖然影評們給這部電影很差的評價，但它的票房還是很好。

　　(A) 評價 (複數名詞)　　(B) 評論 (動詞過去式)　(C) 評論家　　　　　(D) 評論 (現在分詞)

3. Isaac 發現這本雜誌相當吸引人，所以他決定訂閱這本雜誌。

　　(A) 所以　　　　　　　　(B) 雖然　　　　　　　(C) 但是　　　　　　(D) 然後

4. 員工們被經理要求要每天記錄自己的工作進度。

　　(A) 具體說明　　　　　　(B) 要求　　　　　　　(C) 挑戰　　　　　　(D) 質問

5. 這位新銳電影導演非常有才華，她已經得獎兩次了。

    (A) 已經 (現在完成式)　　(B) 是 (過去式)　　　(C) 將　　　　　　(D) 已經 (過去完成式)

6. 總經理已經有一大堆今年和其它公司簽署的合約。

    (A) 收集 (原形動詞)　　(B) 收集 (現在分詞)　　(C) 收集 (過去分詞)　　(D) 一大堆 (名詞)

7. 工作人員需要記錄貨品的庫存數量並確保我們不會供應不足。

    (A) 即將　　　　　　　(B) 變得　　　　　　　(C) 成長　　　　　　(D) 促使

8. 雖然有時候他工作壓力非常大，但他還是能夠應付得過去。

    (A) 因為　　　　　　　(B) 雖然　　　　　　　(C) 儘管　　　　　　(D) 是否

9. 剛發表的數據和我們公司目前的財務狀況相符。

    (A) 相符　　　　　　　(B) 信件　　　　　　　(C) 相符的　　　　　(D) 特派記者

Unit 6

I. Warm-up

Wed.	**Thu.**	**Fri.**
9:00 a.m. visit to GoodBaby Food 12:00 p.m. lunch with Mrs. Coco Melzer		8:00 a.m. weekly meeting 10:00 a.m. meeting at BodyCare Food Building A, Room 308
7:30 p.m. dinner with family at Italian Mama	2:00 p.m. meeting with Mr. Donald go to the baseball game	1:00 p.m. meeting at BodyCare Food Building A, Room 305 2:00 p.m. meeting with Mr. Donald

老闆早安！BodyCare Food 的 Gibson 小姐今天上午早些時候打電話來通知您關於這週五會議時間的調整。會議將會從早上十點開始，而非下午一點。開會地點也從 BodyCareFood 公司 A 大樓的 305 會議室改到 308 會議室。除此之外，我重新安排了您和 Donald 先生的會議，從這週四的下午兩點改成這週五的下午兩點。這樣您週四將會有完整一天的休假。您就可以在那天下午去看令公子的棒球比賽。如果您對我的這些調整有任何問題的話，可以直接打手機給我。

II. Reading

Alvin：我聽說你們要搬去比較大的辦公室了。

Elmore：對啊。我們請了很多新員工。Global Enterprise 正快速成長。

Alvin：的確。我想它很快就會成為世界上位居領導地位的公司之一！

Elmore：希望如此！我們都很高興能達成這樣的成就。看到這個榮譽獎牌了嗎？我上星期五在公司的年度頒獎典禮拿到的。

Alvin：恭喜！那表示你的經理對於你在公司的貢獻有正面的評價！

Elmore：嗯，我非常認真去做每一項我被指派的工作，因為我心中有一個目標。

Alvin：什麼目標？

Elmore：榮譽獎牌得主的獎金！

Elmore：嘿，Alvin！
Alvin：嗨，Elmore！過得如何啊？
Elmore：我剛考核完新進員工的工作表現。雖然他們之中有些人是沒有經驗的，但他們真的很認真工作。你呢？一切都還好嗎？
Alvin：嗯，我們有一個經理忽然提交辭呈，離開了公司。我們很震驚。我們現在忙著處理他留下來的工作。
Elmore：真遺憾聽到這個消息。這是為什麼你看起來這麼疲憊的原因嗎？
Alvin：不完全是。我這幾天牙齒痛得很厲害。我現在得走了，不然我跟牙醫的預約要遲到了。
Elmore：保重！再見。

III. Tasks

1. His company has hired more employees.
2. A medal of honor.
3. He wants the incentive payments for the winner of the medal of honor.
4. He is busy handling the work one of his managers left behind after resigning.
5. He is having a serious toothache these days.

IV. Test Tactics

聽力腳本

Questions 1 through 3 refer to the following excerpt from a meeting.

Welcome to today's meeting. Let's kick off by introducing our future business plans and projects. Firstly, I would like to inform you of our plan to invest $40,000,000 in the Philippine **real estate** market. We've found that the market is starting to flourish. And we will certainly get a high return on this investment. Secondly, we have decided to set up a construction company in Manila which can work **independently** on large construction projects. Lastly, I'd like to confirm the resignation of our assistant manager, Mr. Blake. He will leave next week. Also, the associate general manager, Mr. Ryde, will receive a promotion as a reward for his **contribution** to our company. And Mr. Johnson will be his **successor**.

請參考以下的會議摘要回答第 1 題至 3 題。

歡迎來參加今天的會議。讓我們從介紹我們未來的商業計畫跟專案開始吧。首先，我想告知你們我們在菲律賓房地產市場投資四千萬的計畫。我們發現這個市場正開始蓬勃發展。我們將會在這項投資中得到很高的利潤。再來，我們已經決定在馬尼拉設立一家可獨立執行大型建案的建設公司。最後，我要證實我們襄理 Blake 先生的辭職。他下個星期將會離開。除此之外，我們的副總經理 Ryde 先生將得到晉升，做為他對我們公司貢獻的回報。而 Johnson 先生將會成為他的繼任者。

Questions 4 through 6 refer to the following telephone message.

Hi, Mr. Branton. This is Ryan calling from the manufacturing department. Today we received an order of auto parts that really makes me concerned. There are fewer parts in the boxes than we ordered, which will cause a delay in production. We can't keep manufacturing our cars until we receive the right number of auto parts. I have contacted the supplier, and I would greatly *appreciate* it if you could *transfer* this issue onto our general manager. If there are any problems regarding this issue, please arrange an appointment with him and then we will be able to discuss how to solve it as soon as possible.

請參考以下的電話留言回答第 4 題至 6 題。

Branton 先生您好。我是製造部的 Ryan。今天我們收到了我們訂的汽車零件，這讓我很擔心。包裹裡的零件數量比我們訂的還要少，這會造成生產上的延誤。在我們收到正確數量的汽車零件前，我們無法繼續製造汽車。我已經跟供應商聯絡了。如果你能把這件事傳達給總經理，我會非常感謝。假如這件事情有任何問題，請安排我和總經理會面，我們就能夠盡快討論如何解決這個問題。

題目關鍵字	關鍵訊息
department	➡ This is Ryan calling from the manufacturing department.
problem	➡ There are fewer parts in the boxes than we ordered, which
delay	will cause a delay in production.

4. ___A___ 5. ___C___ 6. ___A___

聽力腳本

Questions 7 through 9 refer to the following talk.

George Canny, our guest speaker, started his career as a real estate investor right here in Cambodia. During the twenty years of his career, he has developed amazing *expertise* in the field of real estate development and investment. He is portrayed by many to be an *authority* in the field of property sales. Recently, Mr. Canny has offered to talk on the topic of how and when to invest in international real estate. It's a great honor to have him as our speaker. I'm hoping that we can all learn from his dedication as an entrepreneur. On behalf of our company, I'm pleased to welcome George Canny.

請參考以下的發言回答第 7 題至 9 題。

我們的特邀演講者 George Canny 就在柬埔寨這裡以不動產投資者的身份開始他的事業。在他二十年的職涯中，他已在不動產的發展及投資領域中發展出非常厲害的專業能力。他被許多人說是房地產銷售領域的權威。最近，Canny 先生表示願意發表關於如何投資及何時投資國際房地產的演說。我們非常榮幸能邀請他來當我們的講者。我希望我們都能學習他作為一位企業家的努力精神。我代表我們公司熱烈歡迎 George Canny。

題目關鍵字	關鍵訊息
purpose of this talk	➡ George Canny, our guest speaker, started his career as a real estate investor right here in Cambodia.
George Canny expert at	➡ expertise in the field of real estate development and investment
Canny's speech about	➡ talk on the topic of how and when to invest in international real estate

7. ___B___ 8. ___D___ 9. ___A___

V. Learn by Doing

1. B 2. C 3. A 4. A 5. B 6. C 7. A 8. B 9. D

聽力腳本

Questions 1 through 3 refer to the following message.

Hello. This message is for Mr. Usher. This is Rocket from K&G Auto Parts. I'm making this call to inform you that the gearbox you ordered the other day is currently not in stock, so we will have to wait until the parts are transferred from our main store. This will take exactly four working days. After fitting it into your car, you will be able to pick up your car. Please come by on Friday morning at 10:00 and pay the bill for the gearbox and repairs done to your car. Thank you and have a good day, sir.

請參考以下的留言回答第 1 題至 3 題。

您好。這是給 Usher 先生的留言。我是 K&G 汽車零件公司的 Rocket。我打電話來是要通知您，前幾天您下訂的變速箱目前正缺貨中，所以我們必須等我們總店調貨來。這會需要剛好四個工作天。在將變速箱裝入您的車子後，您就可以來取車。請在星期五早上十點來，並支付您的變速箱及修車的錢。謝謝。祝您有個美好的一天。

1. 說話者最可能在哪裡工作？
   (A) 藥局　　　　　　　(B) 汽車零件商店　　　(C) 家具工廠　　　　　(D) 醫院
2. 說話者提到什麼問題？
   (A) 藥賣完了。　　　　　　　　　　　　(B) 汽車零件跟車子合不起來。
   (C) 變速箱缺貨中。　　　　　　　　　　(D) Usher 先生將必須再等一個月。
3. Rocket 指示聽者去做什麼？
   (A) 來店裡付款　　　(B) 再等一週修理　　　(C) 去別家店　　　(D) 買另一款變速箱

Questions 4 through 6 refer to the following broadcast.

And now for the TPC Community Bulletin Board. Lillian's Club has announced that the club will be hosting and sponsoring a blood donation activity on Friday and Saturday, July 17th and 18th. The event calls for all who are willing to save lives by donating blood. It will be held in the city hall, near the front gates. Only those with no heart conditions or cancer are *eligible* to donate blood.

請參考以下的廣播回答第 4 題至 6 題。

接下來是 TPC 社區公告。Lillian's Club 宣布他們將舉辦並贊助星期五和星期六的捐血活動，也就是七月十七日和十八日。這個活動號召任何願意藉由捐血來拯救生命的人們。捐血活動將在市政府的大門附近舉行。沒有心臟病及癌症的人才具備捐血資格。

4. 正在宣布什麼活動？
   (A) 捐血活動　　　(B) 羽毛球錦標賽　　　(C) 嘉年華　　　　(D) 演唱會
5. 活動會在何時舉行？
   (A) 六月十七日和十八日　　　　　　(B) 七月十七日和十八日
   (C) 六月十八日和十九日　　　　　　(D) 七月十八日和十九日
6. 活動會在哪裡舉行？
   (A) TPC 社區　　　(B) Lillian's 俱樂部　　　(C) 市政府　　　(D) 捐血中心

Questions 7 through 9 refer to the following excerpt from a meeting.

Welcome to our annual meeting. Tonight people from our three branch offices in Sydney have come here to learn more about our CEO's business ideas and goals. In this meeting, we will cover three items. Firstly, we are planning to open new stores in Melbourne. Secondly, we're gonna build a network platform for all the branch offices, so that all staff can have reliable access to our central database. Thirdly, thanks to the dedication of our North branch office manager, our company has been able to make an extra $20,000 in annual sales. Let's give them a warm round of applause to say thanks.

請參考以下的會議摘要回答第 7 題至 9 題。

歡迎來到我們的年度會議。今天晚上，來自雪梨三家分公司的同仁們都來到這裡，來更多瞭解執行長的生意想法及目標。我們會在這場會議中涵蓋三個項目。首先，我們計畫要在墨爾本開幾家新分店。再者，我們打算為所有分公司建立一個網路平臺，這樣一來，所有員工都能擁有連結到中央資料庫的可靠途徑。第三，多虧了我們北部分公司經理的努力，我們公司的年度銷售額能夠成長兩萬元。讓我們一起來給他們熱烈的掌聲，感謝他們。

7. 會議的目的是什麼？
   (A) 瞭解總裁的目標
   (B) 討論如何提升銷售額
   (C) 更新網路平臺
   (D) 腦力激盪出新的生意點子

8. 公司計畫在哪裡開新店？
   (A) 雪梨　　　　　　(B) 墨爾本　　　　　　(C) 北部　　　　　　(D) 西部

9. 說話者關於平臺說了什麼？
   (A) 平臺已帶來銷售額的增長。
   (B) 平臺提供上網的途徑。
   (C) 平臺可分析銷售數據。
   (D) 平臺將幫助員工得到資訊。

Unit 7

I. Warm-up

1. 5:45 a.m.　　**2.** Rocky Wu; the departure hall of Terminal 1　　**3.** 7:45 a.m.; 7:45 p.m.　　**4.** 12 hours

收件人：	Owen Ortiz 先生和 Olivia Ortiz 太太
寄件人：	Travel With Me Travel 公司 Ruth Haley
日期：	一月二十五日
主旨：	希臘之旅的行程安排
附件：	行程表

親愛的 Ortiz 先生和 Ortiz 太太：

謝謝您選擇 TWM Travel 作為您的旅行夥伴。這封信是要來跟您確認我們已經為您的希臘之旅做了以下安排。請參見附件的行程表。

您的班機將在一月三十一日的早上七點四十五分起飛。請提早至少兩個小時到機場。我們的代表，也就是這次的領隊 Rocky Wu，將會在早上五點半於第一航廈的出境大廳等候您。他在確認你們的身份後會給你們登機證。

您到達希臘的時間預計是一月三十一日的晚上七點四十五分。飛行時間大約是十二個小時。抵達後，Rocky 將會帶您搭巴士到飯店。

如果您有任何問題，請聯絡我們。祝您有個愉快的旅程！

Ruth Haley

II. Reading

Caesar's 飯店

我們飯店很榮幸能接待您。我們希望住宿期間您會感到非常舒適，並希望您在這裡的住宿能夠達到您的期待。請放心，我們在您住宿期間會全程服務。

我們的飯店位於雅典市中心附近。16、21、258 及 655 路公車都會停我們飯店且會經過市中心，班距是十五至二十五分鐘。如果您想搭計程車去市中心、預約餐廳或是訂歌劇門票或電影票的話，請聯絡前臺，我們很樂意協助您。

Caesar's 飯店提供的娛樂設施和設備包含了游泳池、網球場、健身中心、投幣式自動販賣機、豪華酒吧、餐廳等等。歡迎您多加利用。

如果您有任何疑問，歡迎聯絡我們。祝您有一趟難忘的希臘之旅，並希望未來我們能有許多機會再服務您。

飯店經理 Michael Porter

III. Tasks

| 1. C | 2. F | 3. B | 4. E | 5. A | 6. D |

V. Learn by Doing

| 1. C | 2. D | 3. A | 4. D | 5. B | 6. A | 7. B | 8. C |

請參考以下的文章回答第 1 題至 4 題。

Brooklyn 航空公司又再次惹上麻煩。今天，兩位空服員和一位乘客爭執的影片在網路上瘋傳。很明顯的是，那班航班超額預訂。報到的乘客人數超過了機上空位的數量。航空公司為了在機上發生的事情對所有乘客發表了道歉聲明。所有的乘客都得到了該航空公司的機票折價券。然而，許多乘客對於折價券有效期間只有六個月表達了他們的不滿。很多乘客並沒有在那麼短的期間內又有旅遊計畫。

1. (A) 超額預定 (原形動詞) (B) 超額預定 (第三人稱單數動詞)
   (C) 超額預定 (被動式) (D) 超額預定 (進行式)
2. (A) 免費的 (B) 使用中的 (C) 有用的 (D) 可購得的
3. (A) 然而 (B) 具體來說 (C) 否則 (D) 此外

4. (A) 每位乘客都應該得到折價券。

   (B) 影片可能會變得更受歡迎。

   (C) 他們認為應該要有更多空位。

   (D) 很多乘客並沒有在那麼短的期間內又有旅遊計畫。

請參考以下的電子郵件回答第 5 題至 8 題。

收件人：	Allison von Franck
寄件人：	booking13@happytravel.com
日期：	十月二十二日
主旨：	班機和飯店
附件：	時程表；飯店介紹

親愛的 Franck 小姐：

謝謝您對於機票票價及住宿的詢問。來回機票票價是一千三百四十二元。請參閱附件的航班時程表，以確定這符合您的需求和行程。而關於飯店的部分，有很多不同類型的飯店可以選擇，看您是想住在市區、海邊還是靠近山區。請見第二個附件。您可以好好考慮，看哪家飯店最適合您理想的假期。

請儘早回覆我們，以便我們為您安排預約。如果您有任何問題，請寄電子郵件給我。我們樂意為您服務。

5. (A) 儘管　　　　　(B) 至於　　　　　(C) 因為　　　　　(D) 在⋯之中
6. (A) 請見第二個附件。　　　　　(B) 我們有關於當地餐廳的資訊。
   (C) 您應該選擇海邊的渡假村。　　　　　(D) 您何不試試看山邊的小屋？
7. (A) 渴望 (原形動詞)　　　　　(B) 被期望的 (過去分詞)
   (C) 渴望 (現在分詞)　　　　　(D) 渴望 (第三人稱單數動詞)
8. (A) 旅程　　　　　(B) 娛樂設施　　　　　(C) 預約　　　　　(D) 設計

Unit 8

I. Warm-up

Mr. Webb should press ____5____ to reach Ms. Rodgers.

您好，這裡是 Humphreys 製造公司。感謝您的來電。很抱歉，現在我們所有的代表都在忙線中。請稍待一會。我們將會儘快接聽您的電話。如果您知道您要聯絡的分機號碼，請現在撥打。管理部，請按 1。會計部，請按 2。人事部，請按 3。倉儲部，請按 4。業務部，請按 5。行銷部，請按 6。總機，請按 0 或在線上等待。提醒您，我們的辦公時間是週一至週五，從上午九點鐘到下午六點鐘。謝謝您的來電，祝您有個美好的一天。

II. Reading

在地每日新聞

Metalix 金屬公司擴張疆域

　　美國最大的金屬公司之一，同時也是應用最新技術的 Metalix 金屬公司 (以下簡稱 MMC)，週一在賓州開了第八家工廠。

　　MMC 有著獨一無二的行銷網路，並供應產品給遍布在十六個國家超過八十家客戶。它的快速擴張對市場分析師而言並不意外，因為他們從這家公司 2006 年設立以來，早已預測了這家公司可能的成長。

　　MMC 最近取得了一些新產品的專利。執行長 Lee Welch 在星期一的訪談中提到：「我們一直試著開發新產品並改善原有的產品。我們熱切希望能理解客戶並滿足客戶需求，而正是如此的心志促使我們創新。」

　　MMC 已經在金屬產品設計比賽中贏得許多獎項。他們總是能運用最新科技，而且他們的產品都是以環保的方式製造。Lee Welch 說：「新科技的應用已經幫我們減少用水量和用電量，同時也減少了污染。」

　　新工廠的開張讓賓州的部分居民感到不滿。他們不想住得離工廠那麼近。儘管如此，大多數居民還是很歡迎這家工廠的到來，因為它已經帶給當地居民數百個工作機會。

III. Tasks

2. MMC expands rapidly and supplies more than 80 customers in 16 countries.

3. MMC has taken out some patents on their new products recently.

4. MMC uses the latest technology and an eco-friendly way to make products.

5. Most of the residents in Pennsylvania welcome the new plant due to the jobs it has brought.

　(答案僅供參考)

V. Learn by Doing

> 1. C　2. B　3. A　4. D　5. A

請參考以下的廣告、資訊欄和電子郵件回答第 1 題至 5 題。

GLOBAL 健身中心假期特惠

讓身體變得強健成為您的新年新希望

我們在這裡幫您實現

從現在到跨年前，Global 健身中心正舉辦所有會員資格的特惠活動。舊會員購買一年以上的會員資格都打八折。而針對您介紹來的新會員，我們提供七折的優惠！

跨年當天來參加我們的年度跨年慶祝活動吧！全部設備都開放給所有會員，包括會員資格從一月一日才生效的新會員。我們下午六點開門，而這場派對會持續到凌晨四點。

在跨年當天及新年的第一週，不論您的會員等級，我們所有的個人教練都會在現場提供免費諮詢服務。

Global 健身中心 會員資格

效期	健身	游泳池	個人教練
一個月	$35	$10	$15
三個月	$85	$25	$35
六個月	$150	$40	$60
十二個月	$250	$65	$100
兩年	$400	$110	$160
三年	$550	$140	$200
五年	$800	$200	$310

* 一個月的會員資格僅限新會員購買

收件人：	servicedesk@globalgym.com
寄件人：	jsekelow@kmail.com
日期：	十二月十七日
主旨：	關於新年特惠

我已經是 Global 健身中心的會員了，我女友也想成為會員。目前我打算再買兩個會員資格，一個給我自己，另一個當做聖誕禮物給我女友。看到你們的廣告後，我很高興知道我能得到免費諮詢，並且我要買的這兩個會員資格都享有折扣。但是新的會員資格要在一月一日才生效。我想知道我女友是否可以從下午六點開始參加跨年派對，還是她必須等到凌晨才能進去。

非常感謝你。

J. Sekelow

1. 為什麼 Sekelow 先生要寫信給健身中心？
   (A) 為了投訴
   (B) 為了申請職位
   (C) 為了詢問有關一場活動的事
   (D) 為了弄清楚優惠的金額

2. 關於 J. Sekelow，何者不正確？
   (A) 他想買兩個會員資格。
   (B) 他在十二月底的時候看到這則廣告。
   (C) 他可能會和他女友一起參加派對。
   (D) 他女友的會員資格享有優惠。

3. 如果 Sekelow 先生想買兩年的健身會員資格給他女朋友和他自己，他需要付多少錢？
   (A) 六百元
   (B) 六百八十元
   (C) 七百二十元
   (D) 八百元

4. 在這則廣告中，第三段第一行的 complimentary 意思最接近於
   (A) 有限的
   (B) 方便的
   (C) 高品質的
   (D) 免費的

5. Sekelow 先生沒辦法購買哪種會員資格？
   (A) 一個月
   (B) 十二個月
   (C) 兩年
   (D) 三年